Aashish
1926-2034

a novel by

WarrenHall Crain

10 September 2006

© Copyright 2006 WarrenHall Crain.
All rights reserved. No part of this publication may be reproduced, stored in a retrieval system, or transmitted, in any form or by any means, electronic, mechanical, photocopying, recording, or otherwise, without the written prior permission of the author.

Note for Librarians: A cataloguing record for this book is available from Library and Archives Canada at www.collectionscanada.ca/amicus/index-e.html
ISBN 1-4120-9982-x

Printed in Victoria, BC, Canada. Printed on paper with minimum 30% recycled fibre.
Trafford's print shop runs on "green energy" from solar, wind and other environmentally-friendly power sources.

Offices in Canada, USA, Ireland and UK

Book sales for North America and international:
Trafford Publishing, 6E–2333 Government St.,
Victoria, BC V8T 4P4 CANADA
phone 250 383 6864 (toll-free 1 888 232 4444)
fax 250 383 6804; email to orders@trafford.com

Book sales in Europe:
Trafford Publishing (UK) Limited, 9 Park End Street, 2nd Floor
Oxford, UK OX1 1HH UNITED KINGDOM
phone +44 (0)1865 722 113 (local rate 0845 230 9601)
facsimile +44 (0)1865 722 868; info.uk@trafford.com

Order online at:
trafford.com/06-1739

10 9 8 7 6 5 4 3 2

Dedicated to Auntie Sis, my *bua,* my father's sister, who was often a mother to me, as many *buas* are to their brother's children. Would that she could enjoy this novel now.

WarrenHall Crain
10 September 2006

My life is my message.

Gandhi-ji

He was a man, take him for all in all,
I shall not look upon his like again.

Shakespeare
Hamlet I.2.187-188

Contents

Title

Dedication

Gandhi and Shakespeare Quotes

Contents

Introduction (Anil 10 Sept 2035)

The Birth of the Boy (*Bua* 10 Sept 1926)

Most Likely (*Bua* 2 May 1943)

The Wedding Night (Aashish 16 May 1947)

Letter to Tulsa (Aashish 20 May 1947)

Ps to Tulsa (Aashish 20 May 1947)

Reeling from the Horror (Aashish 19 Aug 1947)

Birthday Poem (Aashish 10 Sept 1947)

Summary of 1947-1982 (Anil 10 Sept 2035)

The Old Priest (Aashish 21 Feb 1960)

The Evening Star (Aashish 23 Aug 1965)

Clean Water from the Well (Aashish 4 Jan 1972)

Two of the Fairest (Aashish 23 July 1978)

Glorious India in the Moonlight (Aashish 4 Dec 1979)

Tulsa's Rage (Tulsa 10 July 1982)

The Night on the Roof (Aashish 2 July 1977)

Aashish's Response (Aashish 10 July 1982)

Silly Girl (*Bua* 11 July 1982)

Tulsa's Return (Aashish 11 Sept 1982)

Tulsa's Return (*Bua* 11 Sept 1982)

Bua's Death (Aashish 11 Feb 1988)

The Day Begins in Italiaraja (Aashish 19 May 1996)

The Old Farmer (Aashish 21 August 1997)

Noisy Country (Aashish: 5 Oct 2001)

Devotion (Aashish 8 March 2003)

The Strangeness of America (Roger 1 Nov 2004)

Mister Chief Minister (Aashish 15 Aug 2005)

Such Beautiful Countries (Roger 28 Sept 2005)

An Incident on the train (Aashish 15 December 2005)

Kanniyakumari (Aashish 17 Dec 2005)

Think Globally, Act Globally (Aashish 11 Feb 2011)

We Won (Anil 10 Sept 2016)

Keynote Address (Aashish 14 Feb 2018)

Comment on the Keynote (Anil 21 Feb 2018)

Tulsa's Death (Aashish 16 May 2024)

Nuclear Free Earth (Anil 6 Aug 2028)

Dedication of Janata Mandir (Anil 21 Mar 2033)

Always (Kiran Verma 21 Mar 2033)

Father's Death (Anil 10 Sept 2034)

WarrenHall Crain

from Anil's Journal
10 September 2035

"Nobody in the family was more excited than I in the birth of the boy." This sentence, the first from the first selection I'm including from *Bua's* journal, is a tersely prescient and appropriate introduction of Aashish Kumar Chhaturvedi, my beloved Father.

I've spent many hours and days in this past year since Father's death compiling and selecting and preparing for publication his journal spanning the years from his marriage to our beloved *Mata-ji* right to the evening of her death. As you'll discover in reading this remarkable journal we always used the Hindi term in referring to or speaking with Mother, though we used a formal English term for Father, never *Pita-ji* and certainly not Dad or Papa.

Bua was known as *Bua* by everyone, not only by those of us, my sister and I, to whom she really was *bua,* our Father's sister. I never heard her called by her name, Indira, and I suspect that there were many there in Alimabad and in Bundelnagar who did not even know her name.

Everyone knew her. Many knew her as the town busybody, though she was not thought of harshly or disparagingly. She went about the many often frenetic activities which earned her this epithet with a hearty laugh and a warm smile which demonstrated her genuine love and respect for people. Everyone loved her.

She was tall, as a Punjabi woman should be, though we were not Sikhs. Her face a bit angular and sharp, the sharpness softened by her seemingly ever-present smile. Her hair, of course, black, and worn long in one braid at the back. Her eyes twinkling. Her mouth a bit difficult to describe as she was always talking and I rarely, indeed almost never, saw it still. She was always impeccably dressed in *salwar-kamize*, fiddling all the time with her *dupatta*. I asked her once why she did not adopt the wearing of a *sari* after we had fled to India. Her reply, uncharacteristically terse, "I'm a Punjabi."

She was thin. Many wondered about this as she lived in a prosperous family and well-to-do women in India often show their prosperity by their corpulence. I don't think that *Bua* consciously attempted to keep her weight down. It was just that she was so busy flitting from here to there (as you'll see in a page or two when I stop rambling about her and let you get on to reading her journal) that she did not take time for meals. And even when she did sit down to a meal she was talking too much to have time to eat. She was not, as some suspected because of her thinness, suffering from any illness. On the contrary, she lived her life in the pink of good health.

She raised two children of her own – a boy and a girl, our cousins (though, as is common Indian practice we simply referred to them as our brother and sister, of course using nicknames of various sorts over the years of our growing up). We were in her home as much as in ours and she was as much a mother to us as our own *Mata-ji*, especially after we lost *Mata-ji* in the horror of our flight from the Punjab at the time of the Partition. Though she might not even have understood the term, she was a child development specialist. One of the very best, though not academically trained. She simply was good with people and especially with children. So it is appropriate that her excitement "in the birth of the boy" surpassed that of everyone else.

Her journals written in Punjabi and Hindi and English are extensive. All in finely bound high quality books and written almost always with fountain-pen. None that I have found in simple school-girl notebooks. Her style (you'll see this soon enough, and will be pleased to know that I have been ruthless in editing her entries down to manageable length) flowery, redundant, ebullient, mirrored her life. Her journals were a joy to read. I hope someday to publish them separately so that you can also enjoy their effervescence. I've chosen for this book only those sections which give light to her brother's life.

Enough of introduction. *Bua* often finds her way into Aashish's journal. They loved each other fiercely. Here, then, is the first entry from *Bua's* Journal.

- - - - - - - - - - -

Salwar-kamize -- Punjabi woman's pant suit
Dupatta -- fine long scarf worn across the shoulders

Aashish

Bua's Journal: 10 September 1926

Nobody in the family was more excited than I in the birth of the boy. A fine, strapping Punjabi lad, bawling almost before he had come out of his mother's body far enough that we knew he was a boy. The midwife was very pleased with the progress of this labour and I was jumping up and down in my excited excitement like a school-girl. He is surely going to be our Prime Minister someday, and one of the very best, too. If we ever throw the *ferengi* out and get our independence from the bloody *Angrez*. Of course, his father will have taken care of all of that, working as he does with Jinnah and Nehru and Gandhi-ji and Patel. They'll have this country free long before this boy comes of age. Aashish – I do so hope that Motilal and Khushbu will keep the name I've chosen for this lovely boy – will be in the leadership in building India into a strong and developed nation, enjoying the fruits of the labour of this abundant land rather than giving all away to those hated British. Rest assured, this boy will have none of pandering to our former occupiers, he'll be no namby-pamby, though I do hope that he will help us maintain continuing good relations with them. He will emulate *Bapu* in that.

    Our family has lived in the Punjab now for three generations, since Motilal's grandfather moved here from Central Provinces in search of more fertile land. We have prospered here. Our fields are lush green in springtime and glowing with golden wheat at harvest time. Our orchards produce seers of fruit for market – guava and mango and sweetlime, papaya and banana. We're even experimenting with Punjabi varieties of orange, though we well know that the best oranges grow in Nagpore. And we are having some small success with apples though everyone knows that apples grow best in Shimla's cooler climate. In the vegetable garden brilliant red tomatoes hang heavy like garlands on the plants. Our cabbages are the size of a man's head. Squash and gourds of many sorts lie on the ground and beans climb high on stakes while grapes hang full from the arbours over our heads. Our good Muslim neighbours quote the Koran's descriptions of Paradise when they praise our garden.

Oh, we're not rich folks. That sort live in the cities – in Lahore and Amritsar and Ludhiana. And we rarely go there. We feel uncomfortable there in the hustle and bustle, the crowds, the noise. For us even our district town is too busy. Our home is here in Alimabad. We're village people, prosperous landowners, but village people. Our neighbours here – Sikh and Muslim and Hindu – feel the same. This is our place. This village, like millions of others here in India, is our place. Here we belong.

But I was telling you about the boy, about Bubu. And who am I telling this to? This is my own journal. Who knows who, if anyone, will ever read these words? I'm writing this for me, an ordinary village woman, Bubu's *bua,* his father's older sister. I know that this boy is special and that he will be special not just in my eyes. He is going to be a prominent person not just for our family. Not just for Alimabad. But for all of India. He will be widely known. I hope that he will be one of our country's leaders after we throw the bloody *ferengi* out. Perhaps my small journal will help others to know him better.

I wrote a poem about him today:

> **A boy was born to Motilal**
> **Today a boy was born**
> **A bawling baby came today**
> **Early in the morn**
>
> **So Khushbu smiles**
> **And Prieti laughs**
> **As Bubu cries and sleeps**
>
> **His *bua* knows**
> **That he will be**
> **A man profound and deep**

The boy (I do hope they keep the name "Aashish.") was born this morning at about nine after a not too difficult labour of about sixteen hours. He was crying so lustily that he woke his four-year-old sister. Oh, we all love Preiti. Even the birth of the boy will not diminish our love for his elder sister. But in our traditional Hindu family a son is special. I know that he is a blessing not just for our family and village but for all of India. The astrologers have said so and, even more importantly, in my own heart I feel this. Khushbu is a strong Punjabi woman. I'd expected her to come through this delivery with no major difficulties. She is now resting well and others in the family are caring for her and seeing to all of her needs and his. I've got work to do. Now that we know it's a boy. We've got to arrange his marriage.

Of course, if he was a girl, things would be different. I'd have been waiting on tenterhooks for someone to approach me with an offer of marriage. As he is a boy I can take the initiative. And I know just the family – the Tivaris. Heaven knows I've dropped enough hints in that home that they'll be expecting me now. Sarita or her mother will be preparing the *chai* already in preparation for my appearance. What a lovely family Sarita will have. Sarita is fourteen, she'll be married soon. And her first girl will be promised to Aashish. I hope she has a girl first. Let's see, if she marries in a couple of years , her first child will be about three years younger than Aashish – perfect. Sarita and her parents will be almost as pleased as I in the birth of the boy.

I jotted those notes down before I went to see them and have now copied them into my journal. They were pleased. The marriage is all but finalized. I wonder what her name will be. I'd like Tara, though that name is a bit over-used. Perhaps Sadhana or Aradhana or Chetna. Something which will go well with the name I've chosen for Motilal and Khushbu's boy. They'll have such a fine marriage. Their names should reflect that. Perhaps I should suggest "Tara." I managed to restrain myself this morning and not be so forward as to be seen as pushy. During Sarita's pregnancy I'll have plenty of time to see that her girl is well named.

Aashish

Our family astrologer was not very pleased to see me this morning, though he was not at all surprised. He had heard already about the birth of the boy and he knows me well enough to know that I would not let this day end without tying up the boy's marriage. I tried to persuade him to select the date, but he only laughed and told me that we had plenty of time for that. He also reminded me that we needed to know the exact time and date of the girl's birth. Even I could not give him that, though I've already chosen her name and I know her family well.

I bought some *mitthai* in the bazaar and went to temple. Oh, I know, I should have gone there first. Shri-Ganesh was probably not pleased that I spent all of that time tying up the marriage details before bowing before him. Though I of course had acknowledged him in my own *puja-ghar* right after the birth of the boy, and I had already been to temple earlier in the morning. Our pujari was there – surprising, as it was the middle of the day. So I received his blessing and offered the *mitthai* as *prasad*. He, too, had heard of the birth and was pleased. Our family is well known in our small town and well respected and liked. There was nobody else in the temple, so after I received our *pujari's* blessing he and I chatted about the birth and about our hopes and expectations for the boy. Aashish – surely they'll give him that name -- will come to temple every day and will be trained in the scriptures. Though, of course, he will not be a *pujari* himself, but a politician, an eminent one, a political figure of some renown who will be in the forefront of building independent India.

The day ended for me with another visit to our lovely boy. What a sweet boy he is. Sleeping soundly now in the other room with his mother and father. All is well in this home. Our boy has been born. All is well.

----

10 September 2035: I've cut only a bit of *Bua's* journal at this point and have re-arranged nothing. This journal entry is characteristic, as you will see, of her writing. Anil

----

ferengi – a slightly pejorative word for "foreigner"
Angrez – English
Bapu – literally "Father," Gandhi-ji is often referred to as "*Bapu.*"
mitthai – sweets
puja-ghar home altar or worship space
pujari – worship leader, priest
prasad - sweets or snacks blessed by a priest

Aashish

Bua's Journal: 2 May 1943

I knew it! I knew it! My Aashi ! No surprise to me, but I'm very pleased. Jumping up and down pleased. I knew they would label him with the highest they could think of. He showed me the yearbook this afternoon and turned right to the page of "Most likely to…" Of course, I would not have been surprised to see him chosen as "Most likely to succeed" or "Most likely to marry a beautiful girl." That one would of course have been quite appropriate. He will soon be marrying Tulsa – not just a beautiful girl but <u>the most beautiful girl</u>. Tall and slim like me but much more beautiful. I will be so excited when their wedding comes.

No, they did not choose Aashish as "Most likely to succeed" or "Most likely to have seven children" or any one of the usual "Most likely to…s." My Aashi is

"Most likely to become PRIME MINISTER."

Who could be surprised at that?

Aashi has been Head Boy at the Iqbal Public School for Boys his senior year in Lahore. He has acquitted himself regally all this past year. And, of course, his other years there. We knew that he would do well there, and he has. Winning many prizes, particularly in debate competitions. Not so good in science or maths. He has been such a splendid debater. I remember one debate, when he defended the proposition "When we gain independence we should establish a Muslim homeland separate from India." That was just last year, when Gandhi-ji unequivocally demanded that the British Quit India. Jinnah immediately began militating for a separate Muslim state to be called Pakistan. So, here was my Hindu Aashi, in an overwhelmingly Muslim school, taking the Muslim side. His debate coach had urged him to take the negative side, but Aashi is stubborn and was intrigued by the challenge.

That experience, and I was there in the audience beaming at his persuasive speech, his grasp of the situation, his telling arguments, and of course, at his handsome face. That experience showed Aashi's skill as a debater. It also showed his growing openness to different views. He does not think for a moment that India should become two separate countries, though he is strongly a part of the "Quit India" movement, active in the campus arm of the movement.

He won the debate.

He has done so well his four years at Iqbal Public School. He surprised many of his family and friends. Not me, of course. Maybe I am a bit prejudiced toward him. He is, after all, my brother's son. I've known all along that Aashi is perfect. Oh yes, he has been a difficult student at times, but that's just because he is so smart. And yes, I agree, he was a badmash particularly in his last two years in the government school here in Alimabad. But that was just because he was bored and not challenged at all by his lessons. As soon as he went to Lahore he became an excellent student – top student, Prefect, Head Boy, "Most likely to become Prime Minister" – that sort of student. My Aashi. Of course, the best student in the school.

It is late and I'm a bit tired. I've spent the afternoon – after Aashi showed me the yearbook – visiting friends and family. I want everybody in Alimabad to know. Tulsa was even more proud than I, I think. They will be married soon, just four more years, when Aashish has finished his college.

My Aashi:

"Most likely to become PRIME MINISTER."

THE WEDDING NIGHT

(TULSA HAS BEEN urging me to keep a journal. Surely she will not be angry with me for beginning tonight. Ah, she is laughing quietly, pleased, I think, that I am starting my journal on this most auspicious night.)

I am alone at last with Tulsa after the hustle and bustle of the wedding.

A plain *charpai* covered in cotton *khadi* the color of desert sand is across from the door under the window. On an end table to the left of the bed is a kerosene lamp, and a single candle burns on a shelf behind my right shoulder. I am sitting on a chair opposite the bed, about two feet away from my wife. The room is small, with a low ceiling so that the two lights give a dusty glow, inviting perhaps peace or passion. On the wall behind the bed is a poster of Lord Krishna sporting with his beloved *gopis*.

Tulsa is sitting quietly on the edge of the bed. Nobody else is about in the house and outside the open window the lane in front of the house is quiet – that lane which just this afternoon had rung with the happy laughter of friends and family as Tulsa and I placed our handprints on the wall next to the front door. It is night in the village, the night after the days of our wedding, and I think back over the events of these days.

I remember how anxious I was that first night, the night of the groom's reception. I would not even see Tulsa that night. Though that was not so different than the other days and nights of the *shadi.* Her face was always down and covered by the *pallu* of her sari. But I knew that she was the most beautiful woman in town, and I thought back to the day I had first realized her loveliness. So often I'd seen her coming down the steps of the temple, but that day – *Shivaratri* – she and her mother and sisters were dressed in their finest. I knew then that she was going to be a stunningly beautiful woman and I was proud because I knew that one day she would be my wife.

I remember the *barat,* the procession of the groom to her house, and my many friends dancing in front of me. Some were drunk. Others just intoxicated, as I was, with the joy of the occasion. The band was terrible, but loud.

I remember the garlands and the bliss which shone in Tulsa's eyes as I placed a wedding garland round her neck. And then knowing that she saw the same bliss in my eyes as she garlanded me.

I remember *Chacha pujari,* my uncle the priest, who so often throughout the days of the ceremonies broke into a broad smile, as this was not just anybody's wedding: this was the wedding of his favored nephew.

I remember leading my bride seven times round the sacred fire, knowing then that we really were husband and wife.

I remember seeing our names – Aashish and Tulsa – on the wall in the lane for all to see, knowing now that this was not just my house and my parents', but ours, Tulsa's and mine.

I look across at my wife. For many moments, unhurried at this peaceful hour, I gaze serenely at Tulsa's surpassing beauty, her splendid body open to me now. She returns my gaze with acceptance and love and without a hint of embarrassment.

She sits tall and proud this night. In the part of her hair the red *sindhoor* proclaims her a wife – my wife. Her raven black hair falls unfettered about her shoulders and across her small firm breasts. She is adorned only with simple gold earrings, nose jewel, a teardrop red *bindi* and her wedding bangles, those bangles which we will soon break in the passion of our lovemaking. Yet still for long moments I look at her, and she at me.

I, too, am dressed simply, wearing only a white *khadi dhoti,* my arms and chest glistening with sweat, for it is May, the month of marriages, and very hot even late at night. As I reach across to touch her briefly I am pleased that my brown skin, even darkened as it is by working in the sun, is no match for the dark handsomeness of her face, and shaking my head almost in disbelief that this beautiful woman can be my wife.

Tulsa laughs quietly. We have known all our lives that this night would one day come, and now it has come. Soon after her birth my parents and *Bua* had arranged my marriage with her, and I have always known that she is mine, as she has always known that I am hers. We've always been friends, but only in the past two years, as she has come into the full glory of her womanhood, have I seen her beauty. I have never before seen her without clothing.

Even now she has a soft skirt draped around her hips and legs. The dark red cloth accentuates the deep brown of her small body there in the candle and lamp light. Soon that skirt, too, will be lying on the floor and I will see her body for the first time.

And again she laughs. Even on this most solemn night, and in this situation which is completely new to us, she is fully comfortable in my presence, and the love in her eyes reflects the love and admiration I hold for her.

I join her laughter as she reaches to a shelf beside her for the small silver plate which holds the *paan* she has prepared earlier. As she offers the *paan* to me I simply open my mouth and she touches me for the first time as she places it between my lips. She has prepared a *paan* for herself as well and I first touch her as I place it in her mouth.

She puts the plate back on the shelf and I stand and gently pull her up to stand with me. I loosen her skirt as she loosens my *dhoti* and both garments fall to the ground and we are naked together as husband and wife.

In the morning shards of bangles litter the room..

Aashish Kumar Chhaturvedi
16 May 1947
Alimabad, Lahore District

----

charpai – string cot
khadi – homespun
gopis – milkmaids
shadi – wedding
pallu -- end of sari, often pulled over head or covering face

Shivaratri – "The Night of God", annual festival
   honouring Lord Shiva's marriage

pujari -- worship leader

sindhoor – red color in the part of a married woman's
   hair

bindi – beauty mark on forehead

dhoti – common Indian dress for men – covering the
   lower body and legs

paan – chopped betel nut wrapped in a *paan* leaf

20 May 1947 –*MERI PRIYATUM TULSA, meri bibi*, it may seem a bit strange for me to be writing a letter to you this morning. You are right here in our hotel room, still asleep, after our first honeymoon night here in Shimla. Surely I expressed my love for you more than adequately in our lovemaking last night as you also poured out your love for me in our passion together. May we always be fully open to the physical, sexual ways of expressing our love, throughout our married life.

You know, though, that I have always been good with words. Bua has encouraged me so often to write things down – letters to her, poems, essays, even that foolish short story I wrote when I was only eleven. Bua liked it, but I'm glad few others have been subjected to its maudlin melodrama. Oh, I may re-write it some day, making it palatable to adult readers. And some day I do want to write at least one novel. Though short stories might be more my genre. I revel in the stories of Prem Chand and Manto and Hemingway.

And my teachers at Iqbal Public School encouraged me to do more writing. Sharma-ji, my English Literature teacher, thinks I will be a writer of the stature of Ernest Hemingway. We'll see about that. Sharma-ji was particularly pleased with my translation into Hindi of "For Whom the Bell Tolls." And he has urged me to continue my translations of the great Hindi and Urdu story tellers. To bring their work to English readers. I've already done Prem Chand's *"shatranj ke khilari"* ("The Chess Players") and Manto's *"khol do"* (Open Up), two or my very favorite stories. Ranking, I believe, with Hemingway's best.

Perhaps my life work, rather than teaching, will be translating Hindi to English and English to Hindi so that readers both here and there will be able to enjoy – in their own mother tongue – the great literature of both (well really all three – Hindi, Urdu, English) languages. I think I'll be focusing mainly on American readers, so will need to polish my American English. Who better than Hemingway to help me there. I hope to find an American who will help me with reading and sharpening up my manuscripts. Sharma-ji has offered to continue this help in my translations into Hindi. Heaven knows how much I've benefited by his red marks on my course assignments with him. It took three tries, each time carefully reworking those passages he marked, before he and I were fully satisfied with my translation of *"khol do."*

You're still asleep, Tulsa, as I ramble along here. I expect I'll do this often. Writing to you even when we are together. As I did three nights ago back in our village. Please don't tell your girlfriends that I did that on our wedding night. They will be unmerciful in their ribald jesting – questioning my manhood, wondering whether I was too afraid of sex to take you right to bed, as you were gently urging me to do. You were so beautiful there in our room!

I expect that I will continue to write to you – notes like this one. Love notes, of course. All will express my love for you. Though I cannot at this moment – looking at you asleep beside me on the bed – I cannot comprehend how my love for you will grow. How can it become any stronger or deeper? *Bua* tells me that it will, and how can I contradict her. What a gift, if this powerful love becomes even stronger.

I don't expect you to answer these or to write copious notes to me. That is simply not your style. And I surely hope that you will not go through them and mark them with a red pen. Sharma-ji has done quite enough of that and he will do quite enough of that in the future. Just accept my notes. Read them. Treasure them, I hope. They are just one more way for me to express my love for you.

Ah ! you're awake. I'll order some *chai* and toast.

- - - - - - - - - -

meri priyatum Tulsa, meri bibi - My most beloved
    Tulsa, my wife

Aashish

20 May 1947 (PS TO WHAT I wrote this morning, which you've not even read yet): Tulsa, my love. I was going to say something about children just when you woke up this morning.

Now you are out by yourself in the bazaar. *Bua* would be shocked. A married woman – newly married at that – wandering alone in the bazaar of a strange city. I suppose that *Bua* would be chiding <u>me</u>. Indeed, I can almost hear her sharp demand, "Aashish, why aren't you going with your wife? It is not seemly that she goes alone. What will people think? What will people say?" I am sure that you've been the target of her quick tongue more than once. Never in anger, and always in her love for us, but not sparing in criticism. She was not pleased with the ways in which you did what you chose often in contravention of society's accepted practice. You always felt her too protective. You told her that you knew how to take care of yourself. Now she would have me, as your husband, pick up the sort of protection she wanted to demand. Well, I'm not *Bua*.

That said, I miss you already! You've only been gone a few minutes, and I know you'll not be away long. But I miss you. As I expect I always will when you are not in my physical presence. Now don't fret, I'll not hang on to you as I see some new husbands do. I do my own thing. *Bua* has chided me also about my unwillingness to go along with all of society's ways. You'll find me gone sometimes when you wish I was with you.

On a deeper level, we will always be together. You will always be in my heart as I will always be in yours. Our love for each other is more powerful than something which requires physical proximity. Elizabeth Barrett Browning perhaps expressed this best in her sonnet about her love for Robert:

> How do I love thee? Let me count the ways.
> I love thee to the depth and breadth and height
> My soul can reach, when feeling out of sight
> For the ends of Being and ideal Grace.
> I love thee to the level of everyday's
> Most quiet need, by sun and candlelight.
> I love thee freely, as men might strive for Right;
> I love thee purely, as they turn from Praise.
> I love thee with the passion put to use
> In my old griefs, and with my childhood's faith.
> I love thee with a love I seemed to lose
> With my lost saints, -- I love thee with the breath,
> Smiles, tears, of all my life! – and, if God choose,
> I shall but love thee better after death.

Oh yes... children. I got sidetracked again expressing my love for you. Perhaps, maybe, I'm not so sure, but it is possible, I suppose, that I will not get off on this tangent later in our marriage when the novelty wears off. Maybe, just maybe, I will be able to write to you about something without having to turn my note into a love-letter. I hope not. Let me always and in so many ways – "let me count the ways……." – tell you how much I love you.

All right, all right, Tulsa, I'll get back to the point. Children. Do you remember that afternoon about three years ago? We had met on the temple steps after the evening *arati*. We really were quite good about honoring the expectations people had of us. We did not sneak around meeting each other here and there. Well, only a few times.

You asked me, in an offhand manner, almost as if it was only a bit of conversation, having no particular relevance to you, how many children I wanted to have. You knew as well as I that we would soon be husband and wife. This was certainly no secret in our families. *Bua* made sure of that. Her brother liked to recount with a laugh how, straight from mother's side at the day of my birth, she went to your family to fix up my marriage. And a few years later when you were born she bustled over to check you out, making sure that you had all your fingers and toes and reminding your parents that your marriage was already fixed. You were so coy, always pretending that you knew nothing about this arrangement, that you were simply waiting for your family to arrange your marriage. Our whole community knew that you and I were as good as married. You knew that you would be my wife someday, as you are now. Hurray! Or as our friends, the Brits, might say, "three cheers!"

So when you asked me how many children I wanted your response to my answer betrayed you. It was with obvious relief and joy that you heard me say, "Two, a boy and a girl." You quickly tried to cover up and retreat to your supposed ignorance. "Oh," you said, "just what I want myself." As if you had no idea in the world who the father of your two children might be.

We've not talked about names yet. But I think we agree that two boys will be fine, or two girls, or one of each. Though our families expect us to have six or seven, and surely at least one boy. *Bua* will be expecting that we've already begun this task. Don't tell her that we are choosing to wait until later.

Let's talk about names soon. Knowing you, you've probably got some names in mind already. I know I do. Your loving husband, Aashish.

----

arati – celebrative worship in the temple

Aashish

Reeling from the horror

MOTHER AND ANJALI are dead.

How can this be? How can this terror have engulfed us so swiftly? So unexpectedly? How can our neighbors have turned against us? Many who were our friends were in that mob which tore through our home in last night's riot.

Now I have only time to make these few notes. We leave today. The police urge all Hindus to leave what is now the new country of Pakistan. They assure us of safety on the way to India.

Where will we go? We do not know. We know only that we cannot stay here.

Last night late the rioters broke into our house. Perhaps I'll have time in later years to reflect on these ghastly events. Now I am only reeling from the horror of Mother's death and Anajli's, after being brutalized and raped and murdered by people we knew. People we thought were friends. We've known them all our lives. People who are now our enemies.

Bua and Tulsa escaped. They somehow managed to hide in a closet which was not searched by the mob.

Today we leave. Not six of us, but only four. *Pita-ji*, *Bua*, Tulsa, and myself. Even as late as yesterday I might have said something like "*Inshallah* all will be well." Now I will not use a Muslim expression. Though I do pray God's blessing on our journey – *Jai Shri Ram*.

Mother and Anjali are dead..

Aashish Kumar Chhaturvedi
19 August 1947
Alimabad, Lahore District

- - - - - - - - - -

Pita-ji – a respectful address for "Father."

The suffix "*-ji*" is an honourific.

Inshallah - Allah willing

Jai Shri Ram – long live God

BUNDELNAGAR - A birthday poem

**Beneath the skies above,
Firm on the earth beneath,
In this new land,
In this new place,
We'll build our lives.**

THE TEARING OFF of great chunks of India to build a new Islamic state is mirrored in the horror of the deaths of two of our own. We are not, nor can we ever again be, fully whole. The very fabric of our country is weakened. This family, too, is weakened. We are not all here. We did not all come through.

Mother is gone. She who was the great central strength of this family is no more. Yet her strength is with us for she instilled her strength in us throughout our childhood. Perhaps now it is for me to embody that very strength, to live in its power, to make it my own and to be for this family that firm centre which she was.

**Beneath the skies above,
Firm on the earth beneath,
In this new land,
In this new place,
We'll build our lives.**

We've come so far. At first only fleeing the terror which engulfed our native place as hatred rose against any who were not sons and daughters of The Prophet. Running, stumbling, wailing, carrying what little we could, we fled across the new-drawn border into a land we knew not. Learning that the government has made plots of land available for refugees in the state of Kendra Pradesh, in Bundelkhand, in the very heart of India, we have come here.

> **Beneath the skies above,**
> **Firm on the earth beneath,**
> **In this new land,**
> **In this new place,**
> **We'll build our lives.**

Here, in this new place, with thousands of others who also have come for refuge from the Partition of our country, we'll build a new town. We've come from Rawalpindi, from Lahore, from Karachi. Most are city people. Though many, like our family, have come from the towns and villages of that part of Punjab which is now Pakistan. We will learn to live here. We will learn to farm here. We will thrive here. We've already named our new town Bundelnagar and have established our first Nagar Panchayat. Pitaji – no surprise to me – is the first Panchayat Chairman.

Aashish

> **Beneath the skies above,**
> **Firm on the earth beneath,**
> **In this new land,**
> **In this new place,**
> **We'll build our lives.**

Though now we live in tents in a refugee encampment, in years to come Bundelnagar will shine like a jewel with wide tree lined streets and fine homes. Shops and schools. A new temple to Lord Shiva as the centre piece of our town. A lovely temple tank. A hospital which will be a model of primary care and which will be replicated in small places around the world. A university will be established. A centre for culture and the arts will come up to mirror the glorious annual dance festival in nearby Khajuraho. Industries will grow. Our people will prosper. Here we will stay..

Ashish Kumar Chhaturvedi
10 September 1947
Bundelnagar Refugee Camp

----

nagar panchayat – town council

from Anil's Journal

10 September 2035

Father's journal from the year 1947 right to the year 1982 – thirty-five years – is surprisingly sparse. As I read through for the first time and particularly as I read "The Wedding Night" with Father's comment about Mata-ji urging him to keep a journal, I expected many pages. There is hardly more than the four entries which I include here:

> The Old Priest
>
> The Evening Star
>
> Clean Water from the Well
>
> Two of the Fairest

The family settled into the refugee camp at Bundelnagar. A camp of tents provided by the Indian army, just a few kilometres from the beautiful temple town of Khajuraho. Father's vision for Bundlenagar shines through his 1947 birthday poem. As it has turned out many of those dreams were fulfilled in Khajuraho rather than establishing Bundelnagar as a separate town.

Father's college work had been in education. He had received high grades and was planning to teach there in Alimabad. With Partition and the family's move to Bundelnagar, Father found a position in a school in Khajuraho and then spent most of his professional life as principal of that school. He loved the children – not only his own, myself and my younger sister. He loved all the children of the town it seemed. And they loved him. He knew how they were doing in school almost as well as he knew the national cricket statistics. He would often be found praising a child for a particularly good exam score and then frowning at another for missing school.

He was often surrounded by children as he walked in the bazaar. They called him "Mister C." He wanted them to learn and to practice English, so he would not let them call him "Chaturvedi-ji," and he simply was not comfortable with their addressing him as "Sir."

Grandfather had been chairman of the *Nagar Panchayat* in Bundlenagar, and Father was selected as the first *Nagar Panchayat* representative from Bundelnagar when the refugee camp was merged into Khajuraho in 1957, and he served as *Sarpanch* for several terms.

- - - - - - - - - -

Mata-ji – a respectful address for "Mother."
Sarpanch – Chairperson

THE OLD PRIEST

HE SITS SERENELY on the steps of a nearby temple, calmly watching the thousands upon thousands of devotees coming and going from the temple he has served now for more than seventy years. This *pujari* (priest, worship leader) is now eighty-five years old and this morning of the Night of God he has chosen to sit on the sidelines and watch the passing scene. He tells me, waving his arthritic hands, that he is no longer able to do the *puja*. One of his sons and a grandson and many other priests are in and around the Matangeshwar Temple and he thinks back over other *Shivaratri* celebrations in his time of service here.

Always on this day and night immense crowds of people, for on this night we remember the wedding of Lord Shiva and his consort Parvati. Women come dressed in their finest *saris*, but men bathe in the lake nearby and come dripping wet, bringing pots of water to bathe the *lingam*, the great stone shaft in the center of the temple which symbolizes Lord Shiva in the hard passion of intercourse with his beloved Parvati. John the Evangelist said, "The WORD became flesh." So here, we Hindus take this symbol of sexual delight as a sign of God's love for his people and a sign of the bliss (*ananda* in Sanskrit) which is our birthright.

The old priest is filled now with *ananda* as he watches the *bhaktis* (devotees) this morning. His cup runs over.

He was alone when I saw him first, but when I make my way to him to touch his feet and receive his blessing I find him chatting with two tourists. Bliss shines in his warm smile as he welcomes me. He knows, as the psalmist David knew, that he lives in the house of the LORD always.

The old priest is my uncle..

Aashish Kumar Chhaturvedi
21 February 1960
Khajuraho

THE EVENING STAR

Star light, star bright, first star I see tonight,
I wish I may, I wish I might, have the wish I wish tonight.

I saw the evening star tonight
above the temples shining bright,
but no wish had I in my mind
to take advantage of its light.

The emptiness my head did bind
with fears and doubts of every kind.
"Am I without a dream," I cried,
"when hollowness is what I find?

But dreams I have, and visions glide,
of glorious life on every side;
not just for me, but every soul
who lives on this great world and wide,

in every place, from pole to pole;
all life fulfilled, complete and whole..

Star light, star bright, first star I see tonight,
I wish I may, I wish I might, have the wish I wish tonight.

Aashish Kumar Chhaturvedi
23 August 1965
Khajuraho

CLEAN WATER FROM THE WELL

FILLING FIRST THE galvanized bucket and then the perhaps ten litre brass water pot, she adjusts her *sari*, wraps a cloth in a circle for her head, and hoists the brass water pot like a weight lifter, back straight, first to shoulder then up onto the cloth on her head, in two swift, sure, graceful moves. Only then, pot secure on her head, does she, still keeping her back straight, bend her knees, reaching for the bucket, and with consummate grace, begin her walk home.

When she was a child and still learning this supple art she often dropped the pot from her head either as she stooped to pick up the bucket or on her way home. She still keenly remembers the fierce sting of humiliation as others laughed at her clumsiness. But she has never as an adult dropped a pot. Nor has she ever seen another grown woman so humiliated.

Children bathe next to the pump, naked in the warm afternoon sun.

These pumps – tube wells, as we call them here, drawing water from twenty metres down or fifty metres down – are transforming our country. Fresh water easily available close to home means that we keep ourselves and our homes cleaner. Clear, pure water is the birthright of every person and we will pray and work until everyone on this planet has:

> **clean, pure water**
> **enough food to eat every day**
> **a clean, safe place to live**
> **basic education**
> **basic health care.**

This great world has vast resources. We must ensure their equitable distribution to all..

Aashish Kumar Chhaturvedi
4 January 1972
Gursrai

Aashish

TWO OF THE FAIREST

"Two of the fairest stars in all the heaven…" –
Shakespeare

Two of the loveliest girls in all the world
sit one on each side of me,
stringing flower garlands to sell to the tourists,
to supplement their modest family income.

I've known the eldest since she was a little girl.
Now even her mother acknowledges that
Salu is no longer a girl. She is now a woman,
indeed, of marriageable age.
I will myself go next week with her father and
    mother
to the village
to find a suitable boy.

Heaps of flowers at her feet, Salu sits on my left,
dressed in a lime green *salwar kamize.*
Simmi on my right in regal purple.
Salu's hair in a long pony tail,
Simmi's in two pigtails,
bantering as two sisters will
and flashing smiles at me
from time to time.

This whole family,
father, mother, younger sister, elder brother,
two older sisters now married,
are among my closest friends

in this small central Indian town.
I see these two lovely girls every day.

I usually call them "Salu" and "Simmi,"
using their house names.
Now, in acknowledgement, I surmise,
of their own young womanhood,
they ask me to use their proper names,
"Sadhana" and "Aradhna."

Romeo referred to Juliet's eyes as
"two of the fairest stars in all the heaven…"
I know Sadhana and Aradhna as
two of the loveliest girls in all the world..

Aashish Kumar Chhaturvedi
23 July 1978
Khajuraho

GLORIOUS INDIA IN THE MOONLIGHT

I would sing of the glory that is the Taj Mahal,
rising out of the smoke of an Agra evening
into the full light of the moon.

Minarets and dome and inlays sparkling,

And as the pilgrim approaches looming huge.
Yet always delicate and of consummate grace.

So, too, I would sing of India,
of *Maha Bharat,* the land I love,

Rising out of the oppression of generations,
the paternalism of the Raj,
the horror of abject poverty,
the debilitating effects of disease and illiteracy,
into the full light of *Swaraj,*
of self rule by all.

Villages and cities and people sparkling
with new hope and determination.

And as the seeker travels becoming
almost overwhelming in her vast scope.
Yet always delicate and of consummate grace..

Aashish Kumar Chhaturvedi
4 December 1979
Agra

-- written on return to our room at the Taj Khema Hotel after Tulsa and I had seen the world's most beautiful building by moonlight.

Aashish

from Tulsa's journal: 10 July 1982:

How could he? How could he deceive me? He is just like other men. I thought he was different. I thought our marriage was different. Now, after thirty-five years of marriage, I find that ours also fits the stereotype. The dutiful wife stays home while the husband, her LORDANDMASTER, screws around wherever and whenever he pleases.

He claims that this is only a story. Poetic, erotic fantasy, he says. He claims that it never happened. He claims this is only in his imagination. He claims that he has always been true to me. He claims that he has never had sex with another woman. He is just like every other Indian village man. He claims that he is different. He is not.

Well, he'll never have sex with me again. I'm leaving! Back to my village. He can do whatever he damn pleases. I'm through with him.

Here, if you are already reading my personal journal, go ahead and read his story. "Story" he calls it. Guilty confession more likely. Here. You read about "The Night On The Roof"

What can I do?

I AM NOT GOING TO STAY WITH THIS MAN!!!!!!!!

THIS WHOREMONGER!!!!!

BASTARD!!!!!!!

CHEAT!!!!!

FILTHY WRETCH!!!!!!

I'm through. After thirty-five years of marriage, a marriage which I thought was nearly perfect, I find he has deceived me. I'm through. Our marriage is finished.

The Night on the Roof

SHE CAME AND stood quietly in the open door of the room in which I was napping in the heat of the early afternoon. Then came and sat on the bed next to me. Others came and went, but she stayed. Sitting beside me on the bed, her hand from time to time brushed against my outstretched arm. I gazed long at her face. She returned my gaze with no hint of embarrassment. Her smile, lush and full and sensuous, sultry in the warm afternoon, stirred me, and I said to her, *"tum bahut manohar aurat ho,"* "you are a very pretty woman." She simply smiled again and I began to stroke her hand. Did she intend to stir me? Surely she knew that her presence alone with me might arouse me. Was she as aroused as I was?

After some moments she said, *"Iti thik nahin lagta.",* "This does not seem right." Quietly she got up and with a gentle smile brought me a glass of cool water.

She came to me again that night as I slept on the flat roof on stones still warm from the afternoon sun but with air cool enough that I was glad for a light blanket. *Chandrama,* the moon, was full, and Orion and the Great Bear were also my companions in the night sky.

I awoke to find her again sitting beside me, smiling, wearing a simple shift, her long black hair down and free. She placed a finger across my lips to warn me that our lovemaking must be quiet as others in the family were sleeping nearby. She put her finger to her own lips to assure me that no word of this night would leave her mouth. Then she stood and in one swift, graceful movement pulled the shift over her head and stood naked in the moonlight. I gazed for long moments at her smooth, brown body, her firm breasts, her dark pubic hair. The warm, moist lips between her legs beckoned from shadow as the moon was now high in the night sky.

As I raised my arms to draw her down to me her nose jewel flashed in the moonlight and the scent of sandalwood came to me from the sandalwood paste with which she had adorned her breasts. She knelt and loosened the knot of my *lungi* and I lay naked in her sight and, without a hint of embarrassment, returned her broad smile.

How long had it been since I had been in the embrace of a warm, female companion? I could not count the days.

My penis was hard as she caressed me. We kissed and I found her lips willing and eager as I was willing and eager. I stroked her hair and her face, her back and her proud breasts. My hand moved slowly over her long legs and up inside her thighs until my finger slipped between her moist lips. She lay quietly, yet responsive to my every touch, and returned kiss for kiss. She was breathing deeply, yet without a word, as I brought her to the height of her passion. Then she covered my eager body with hers and my penis slipped hard and deep inside her. Her swift, sure, loving movements soon brought me to joyous climax and I was about to cry out in ecstasy when, with a low laugh, she again placed her finger across my lips.

We slept with my penis still deep inside her. How long we slept I do not know, but the Earth and the stars had moved. The Great Bear was in a different place and the moon was lower in the sky.

For long moments still we held each other. I toyed with her long black hair and stroked her face and neck. She held my face in her hands and smiled at me. And again we kissed – now in the tender remembrance of passion spent and received. After some time she reached for her shift and she was gone.

While we lay together the Earth had moved. The Great Bear had wheeled round the polar star and *Chandrama* had smiled on our lovemaking.

The next morning, as with joined palms I said my goodbyes to the family, she warmly returned my *Namaste* and her open smile revealed that she understood when I mouthed the words, *"tum bahut manohar aurat ho.."*

Ashish Kumar Chhaturvedi
2 July 1977
Achnar

a note: The first and last scene actually happened. I've recorded them here with no embellishment. And, though I did sleep on the roof under the full moon, the scene on the roof is a flight of poetic, erotic fantasy. akc

10 July 1982: *MERI PRIYATUM TULSA, meri bibi.* What can I say? What can I do? I have deceived you. Though now you know. I'm not deceiving you now. Though I tried to keep up the deception, claiming it was only a story, not a real incident in my life.

You know me too well to believe that. Now you know that I have been unfaithful to you.

I feel relief that you know. I no longer have to play the charade of the unspotted and unspottable husband. And I feel shame for what I did – now more than five years ago. And I feel anguish bordering on real terror over what the future holds for us and for our marriage. I know you well enough to realize that there may be no future for us. I know your dogged persistence and your steely resolve to live according to your own best understandings rather than the dictates of others. You have told me plainly and clearly that this is the end of our marriage. You may well hold to that resolve. Though I keenly hope that you will not.

I also know your love for me and mine for you. Our love, each for the other, has deepened and strengthened year by year and has never been stronger than it is right now. Few there are who find this depth of love for another human being. I know that somewhere under your intense and appropriate rage you know your love for me and mine for you. My hope is that this love will bring you back to me again.

I will in no way attempt to minimize what I have done. It is a dastardly betrayal of the woman I love. I am guilty of a heinous deed which has lead to months and years of secret guilt and now to a rupture in a marriage which we had both thought near perfect. I had never betrayed you before. I have not since, nor will I. This was a one night affair.

I am sorry for what I have done, Tulsa. I will be faithful to you as long as we both shall live. Your loving husband, Aashish

----

10 September 2035: Though one can never be entirely certain about the private, personal aspects of other's lives, I believe that the "Night on the Roof" was the only time Father strayed outside the bounds of strict sexual fidelity and I believe that *Mata-ji* never did so. Anil

----

meri priyatum Tulsa, meri bibi – my most loved Tulsa, my wife

Aashish

Bua's Journal: 11 July 1982

She had come to me distraught, crying, sobbing, her hair disheveled, no *kum kum* in the part of her hair, no *bindi*, her *sari* torn and carelessly thrown around her. Never, never in all of her life had I seen her in such a state. Something terrible must have happened, I thought. Horrible thoughts came into my head. Has Aashish been murdered? Or Anil? Or does one of them have cancer? Or has their house fallen down? What could possibly make my Tulsa act like this?

She ran into my arms, bawling uncontrollably, and I held her until she began to speak. Angry awful words came one by one and it took me some time to realize that she was angry with her husband. So angry that she had washed the red out of the part of her hair and came to me as if she was not even a married woman. **"Bastard,"** she wailed. **"That son of a bitch,"** came out through clenched teeth. **"Whoremonger."** I never heard such words from Tulsa, my sweet, lovely Tulsa. What is she talking about?

Yes, early this afternoon Tulsa had come to me to finally, after calming herself enough to talk coherently, pour out her troubles. Aashish has been running around with other women, she told me. What?? My Aashi?? My little boy?? Of course, he is not a little boy any more, but to me he is my little boy and this cannot possibly be true. Aashi cannot have done this. Not my Aashish Kumar Chhaturvedi. And I told her sternly to stop talking that way.

She firmly held to her story. She believes that he is running around, that he is not faithful to her. This cannot be true. Not my Aashi. "Stop sobbing and talking like a silly girl. Go home, take a bath, put on a fresh sari, put *kum kum* back in your hair. Tell your husband that you are sorry."

Nothing would do. She hardly listened to me. To me, her *bua*. She held doggedly to her story. She had no husband. That person she had been married to had cut their ties and she was going home to her family. I could not dissuade her. Even after she had calmed down enough to tell me that he had only once been with another woman – hardly the whoremonger she had been shouting about.

"Only once?" I asked, though I did not even for a moment believe that my Aashi had been unfaithful to her even once. But even if this story of hers is true, this is a pretty minor infraction of their marriage contract. There are precious few men, anywhere in the world, to say nothing of Bundelkhandi men, who remain faithful to their wives. Most men run around. But not my Aashi. But even if he had gone out once, I counseled her, this is not the end of the world or the end of your marriage or the end of your happiness. "Go back and tell him you are sorry. *Bas*, finished."

She would have none of my counsel. Never before had I seen her so intransigent, so stubborn. Oh, my Tulsa has always been a headstrong, stubborn girl. But today nothing I could say moved her in the least. She left, not to go back to Aashi, whom she no longer considered her husband. She went back to her family.

I must go talk with Aashi tomorrow. Surely there is some reason his wife is so angry. But surely it is not what she says.

- - - - - - - - - -

Bas – Enough! Stop!
kum kum –red powder which a married woman
      wears in the parting of her hair
bindi – beauty mark on forehead

IT WAS AS if she had never been away. Or as if she had simply stepped out for an hour or so to buy some vegetables for the evening's dinner. I found her in the kitchen cutting the vegetables when I returned home yesterday from my lonely lunch at the Khajuraho Road *Dhaba*.

I had not had a single word from her for two months, since she had read my purportedly fictional account of "The Night on the Roof." And now yesterday I found her here at home and she greeted me as if she had never gone away.

She had written me a scathing response, using language which I never heard her speak in all of our lives together. An appropriate response to my dastardly behaviour. And she had taken her clothes and gone back to her parents, who had also come across to India at the time of Partition and were living near Delhi.

I wrote letters to her. The letters were returned by the post office marked "refused – return to sender." I had sent e-mails. No response at all. I had phoned on several occasions, and even talked with her mother at one point. Her mother had simply, and curtly, told me that Tulsa will not speak to me.

Now she is back. And she has reclaimed our bed where she welcomed me warmly last night. We will surely talk about this later, but now she has come back to me and we are together again.

I wrote a brief note to her early this morning as she lay still asleep in our bed. Handwritten, of course, and in Hindi. This is my translation for my private journal:

Meri priyatum Tulsa, meri bibi, "How do I love thee?" More deeply, surely, and more fully even than Elizabeth Barrett Browning loved Robert. My love for you has never wavered, even in the dastardly betrayal which took you away from me these past two months. And though I know that there is no way in which I can prove my faithfulness yet know that I will not again betray you. In the old-fashioned words of the traditional Christian order of Matrimony (I've had to check this from the Anglican prayer book which my friend Roger gave me long ago.) "I will keep me only unto thee so long as we both shall live."

I am reminded now of another time when I wrote to you. Our wedding night. We were alone together for the first time after the hustle and bustle of the wedding festivities. I thought then that I would never more deeply feel my love for you. I find now that I was wrong. Over the years my love for you has deepened and, looking at you asleep now in our bed, I can say that I've never loved you more completely.

I am deeply sorry, Tulsa, for my betrayal that night in the village. I know that the revelation of that betrayal as you read my supposedly fictional story must have cut like a knife. And I know that there is no way that I can erase that pain. I can only own up to the fact that it was I who caused the pain. My betrayal. My weakness. My wrong. Yes, my sin.

And I know that I will not do this again.

Walking into the house yesterday and finding you here as if you had never left, singing your favorite Bollywood song as you prepared vegetables, was a moment of intense relief to me. I had feared that you would never return. Indeed, I expected that you would not return and that our marriage was at an end. That we would live out our lives apart.

But never once did my love for you fail. And I know that your love for me has never faltered, even though I gave you reason to hate me.

We've known each other all of our lives, Tulsa. And we've loved each other from those early days when it seemed only a childhood romance, though we knew then, of course, that *Bua* had arranged our marriage on the day of your birth.

My love for you will only grow deeper with the years.

Ah, you are stirring. I'll go and make some *chai*.

Tumhara priyatum pati, Aashish

> Aashish Kumar Chhaturvedi
> 11 September 1982
> Khajuraho

----

dhaba – roadside restaurant

tumhara priyatum pati – your most-beloved husband

Bua's Journal: 11 Sept 1982

Nary a word from that silly girl. And now she has come back. As if nothing ever happened. And nobody could be more pleased than I am. Well, Aashi, of course.

I had gone to Aashish the day after his wife had run crying to me. I could not believe that her story was true, but Aashish confirmed that it was indeed true. He had on one occasion, and only one, taken another woman to bed. And, silly boy, he had written about it in his journal, pretending that it was only a story. Tulsa somehow had read it and, knowing her husband intimately, realized that it was not fiction at all. She had confronted him and he had admitted that it was true.

Over the last two months since that awful day when my Tulsa had come sobbing to me, I had tried to reach her so many times. So had Aashi. No response until yesterday – Aashi's fifty-sixth birthday.

It is still hard for me to believe – hard to believe, but true – that my Aashi strayed outside the bounds of his marriage contract.

Never again. He says. And I believe him.

Aashish

MY *BUA* IS gone. I was reading to her. Almost every day I came to the nursing home where she had been living for the past two years. Her health was fine, but each day she seemed a bit weaker, though always alert and happy. I came nearly every afternoon to read to my *Bua*.

On Tuesday she had asked me to read the Twenty-third Psalm from the Christian scriptures – not from the English which we often used but from our mother tongue, Punjabi:

The LORD is my shepherd; I shall want nothing.
He makes me lie down in green pastures,
    and leads me beside the waters of peace;
    he renews life within me,
    and for his name's sake guides me in the right path.
Even though I walk through a valley dark as death
I fear no evil, for thou art with me,
    thy staff and thy crook are my comfort.

Thou spreadest a table for me in the sight of my enemies;
    thou hast richly bathed my head with oil,
    and my cup runs over.
Goodness and love unfailing, these will follow me
    all the days of my life,
    and I shall dwell in the house of the LORD
    my whole life long.

(New English Bible, Thomas Nelson and Sons)

Then yesterday she wanted me to read her favorite passage from the Bhagavad Gita. I did not need the book yesterday. That text, in English and in

Hindi, is in my head. I recited, as she asked, in Hindi, Krishna's words to Arjuna:

Give me your whole heart; love and adore me; worship me always; bow to me only; then you will find me. This is my promise, who love you dearly. Lay down all duties in me, your refuge. Fear no longer, for I will save you from sin and from bondage.

>(The Bhagavad Gita, translated by Eknath Easwaran, Nilgiri Press)

Today, when she asked me to read her favorite poem from Gitanjali, in Tagore's own English translation, I sensed that this might be the last time I would ever read to her, and I was afraid to look up from the page as I read:

Light, my light, the world-filling light,
the eye-kissing light,
heart-sweetening light!
Ah, the light dances, my darling, at the center of my life;
the light strikes, my darling, the chords of my love;
the sky opens, the wind runs wild, laughter passes over
    the earth.
The butterflies spread their sails on the sea of light.
Lilies and jasmines surge up on the crest of the waves of
    light.
The light is shattered into gold on every cloud, my darling,
and it scatters gems in profusion.
Mirth spreads from leaf to leaf, my darling,
and gladness without measure.
The heaven's river has drowned its banks
and the flood of joy is abroad.

>(www.schoolofwisdom.com/gitanjali.html.)

When I looked up from the book she was gone.

Bua was a skeptic, as am I, but we each believe that this earthly life is a part of a much greater life. And now, in *Bua'* s death, "the heaven's river has drowned its banks and the flood of joy is abroad.."

Ashish Kumar Chhaturvedi
11 February 1988
Khajuraho

THE DAY BEGINS IN ITALIARAJA

THE CHILDREN HAVE their baths here in the open courtyard of the village farmhouse. Water is flowing from the tap coming from the new municipal supply in the next village. *Bade bhabhi,* wife of eldest son, mother of three, bathes her children one by one. First three-year-old Jitendre, then my darling Prithi, the pretty five-year-old girl who stole my heart on my previous visit, and then eight-year-old Dharmendre. Each one cries. The youngest because he got soap in his eyes. Prithi because the water is cold. Dharmendre, I suspect, out of embarrassment that I am watching while his mother bathes him. "I'm quite old enough to bathe myself," he is thinking.

We've risen with the sun, having slept on mats spread on the open first and second floor roofs. There are, I think, thirteen people who slept here last night – the master and mistress of the house, eldest son, his wife and three young children, one other son and daughter (teen-agers), second son's wife (her husband is living and working in Khajuraho), a nephew whose house is nearby, another nephew who came with me on this visit, and myself.

The clear strong call of peacocks and peahens from their perches in the highest trees, and the red orb of *Surya* through the branches of those trees, had woken me at sunrise. I had looked around and seen that my host was already up, but fifteen-year-old Anand was still asleep, and five-year-old Prithi, and the three boys. So I closed my eyes again and slept until Prithi called me some time later.

Getting up, I see, down in the street below, my host busy spinning jute twine. Smoke rising from the courtyard gives promise of a cup of chai. And in a few minutes *bade bhabhi* smilingly sets down before me not one but two cups of steaming hot sweet milk tea.

I have my bath, the cold water refreshing after a quiet night's sleep and reminding me of the day's heat soon to come.

Chhoti bhabhi, wife of younger son, literally "little sister-in-law," prepares breakfast over a straw and cowdung fire in the *chulha* in the courtyard.

Others come and go in the normal open style of an Indian home. A young girl takes her bath. Who is she? I don't know. A young boy walks in. Probably relatives from next door. And probably attracted by the water flowing from the tap – one of the few water taps in the village.

This is a home built on the traditional Indian pattern, though this one is larger and more prosperous than most. Two-storey carved cement façade on the narrow dirt street with large elegant wood doors which lead one through two very dark rooms into the inner courtyard, the central focus of the house. In the courtyard a small altar for occasional ceremonies on marriages or other special occasions. A small tree struggling to find its place in the family. The water tap at which the family bathes. In the corner the brick and mud *chulha* where most food is cooked. Open porches on both sides – very pleasant places in the heat of the day. Two more dark, windowless rooms at the back. Two flights of steep stairs, one front and one back, take one up to the wide open first floor roof and two more rooms, these bright and airy with windows on all sides. Then a flight of stairs up to the second floor roof, the top of the house, where we slept.

The heat of the 8AM sun reflected off the house across the street is almost frightening in its intensity. So, I retreat to the cool of the inner courtyard, and in the heart of this family, sit and write. I've already succumbed to heat exhaustion twice this season. Let not today be number three.

And so the day begins..

Aashish

Aashish Kumar Chhaturvedi
19 May 1996
Italiaraja

p.s. An unexpected rainstorm came through right at the heat of the day – about four in the afternoon – giving us a pleasantly cool evening and, while I slept very comfortably under a quilt last night, others either fled the roof during the night to seek warmer quarters indoors or complained about how cold the night had been.

akc
20 May 1996

THE OLD FARMER

TOWEL OVER ONE shoulder, sacred thread over the other, he stands in the doorway in the hazy afternoon sunlight. It has just rained, and the air is clear and fresh. He stands erect and sure, waiting for his daughter-in-law to bring *lota* and bucket and rope so that he can go to the well for his afternoon bath.

He is still handsome at 73. His years in the fields have kept him strong, and today to me, as I watch him in the doorway, he embodies the deep strength of my beloved India, this rich land where sixty per-cent of the people still live in villages.

His white hair is short cropped and he wears a three or four day growth of beard. Most of his teeth are still intact and his smile is full.

He lives here with his son and with his son's wife and daughter, in the assurance of care for the rest of his life.

He owns little – perhaps one good *dhoti* and *kurta* for special occasions. Today he wears only an old *lungi*. His legs and chest and arms bare, firm and fit, in the chocolate-brown skin of the people of this land.

He bathes by the well in the warm afternoon sun.

Aashish

Finishing his bath he draws one more bucket, coils the rope, and takes from the bucket one *lota* of water. Standing by the well side he slowly pours the water back into the well in gratitude and tosses the lota back into the bucket. Then, taking bucket in hand and coiled rope in the other, he strides back to the house, bringing us a rich gift – fresh clean water from the well.

Aashish Kumar Chhaturvedi
21 August 1997
Khajuraho village

----

lota – a small brass container for water or food

dhoti – a single piece of white cloth, draped like trousers, common dress for men, covering the lower body and legs

kurta – a long, formal, shirt

lungi – a single piece of cloth wrapped around like a skirt, usually for everyday, not formal, wear

ROGER, MY FAVOURITE *mantra* these days seems to be "My How I love this country!" Here is just one instance of my use of this *mantra:*

My but this is a noisy country!

*Barats (m*arriage processions) in this town where I am staying for a few days often start in the street in front of the hotel and are always boisterous affairs. Led by a brass band playing at full volume, the band nearly drowned out by the over-amplified synthesized music from the music van which forms the head of the procession. This van decorated with hundreds of flashing colored lights and long fluorescent tubes. The band itself lit up by a line of women carrying tube-light lanterns on their heads. And all energized by a generator on a push cart. This is then followed by the groom on a horse or on a horse drawn cart. All accompanied by a few hundred friends and family, some dancing, some drunk, all festively dressed for this occasion.

I've just described a normal wedding procession – a loud, colorful affair taking the groom to the home of his bride (whom he has probably not yet seen) for the wedding much later in the night.

Tonight however, as part of the *Navratri* (nine night) celebrations for the Goddess Durga, the *barat* is taking the great God Ram for his wedding to Sita

This evening not only one, but three bands were in the procession– each with around one hundred men playing lustily. Seven generators were needed to power this immense procession. The streets were crowded with onlookers, and still normal city traffic had to make its way past the *barat* in both directions. Adding the noise of their horns.

The band leading the procession was "The Super Anand Band." "Super" means the same in English as in Hindi. "Anand" means "Bliss." This noisy procession seemed far removed from any idea I might have had of "bliss." But then, what we are celebrating is nothing less than the marriage of God Himself. Surely an occasion for super bliss.

My how I love this noisy country!

Aashish Kumar Chhaturvedi
5 October, 2001
Jhansi, UP

- - - - - - - - - - -

I do not know exactly when Father's friendship with Roger Marley began, but this is one of several letters explaining Indian customs. Anil

DEVOTION

FOR LONG MINUTES I stood at the base of the wide stone steps leading up to the Matangeshwar Temple here in Khajuraho, on a bright spring morning, watching people come and go.

Am I a spectator? Yes, but more than a spectator. A believer in Lord Shiva? I think not, though I do attend the brief, celebrative *arati* every evening in this temple. I am a devotee, somehow a part of the devotion which is so palpably evident in this place. This has been a holy space now for one thousand years and more. Every day people have walked up and down these twenty-seven stone steps, just as they are doing today. Coming to worship in simple, direct ways: touching the ground and the feet of the idols; pouring water ritually; perhaps bringing flowers; receiving the blessing of the priest. Very little has changed.

Two men come together. Friends, I surmise. *Dhotis* draped around their legs wet from their having just bathed in the lake nearby. Bare from the waist up except for silver amulets on black strings around their necks. Their flat bellies, muscled arms and shoulders, and the darkness of their skin, even darker than the chocolate-brown of others, evidence that they are used to work in the fields. Only their hair shows their age.

One is white-headed. The other almost bald. Each carries a small brass pot full of water to perform *abhishek,* ritual washing of the temple. Each pours a few drops on the steps before starting up, then one at a time they pour water over the statue of Lord Ganesha on the platform halfway up. The rest of the water will be used to bathe the great stone *lingam,* representative of the procreative power of Lord Shiva, which stands three metres tall in the middle of the temple.

Only a few at a time are coming today. Mostly simple people, unlettered, untraveled. People of the land. People of the earth. I see no man wearing the sacred thread. These are lower caste people.

One week ago, on the festival of Shivaratri, commemorating the marriage of Lord Shiva and his consort Parvati, perhaps as many as one hundred thousand people came. Security forces for three days kept the crowds in line. Today one person at a time or groups of four or five go up to the temple.

Women come in *saris* brilliant of every hue. Many young girls come wearing only panties. The older girls in frilly western-style frocks. Men and boys, stripped to their undershorts, come dripping wet from the lake. These are mostly poor, village folks.

But three men come dressed in fine shirts and slacks. Carrying suitcases they go up the steps looking for all the world as if they were going into a fine hotel. Except that they, too, have removed their shoes.

As they go up people touch the steps in reverence then bring their hand to forehead and heart. As they leave, at the bottom of the steps, many turn and place their forehead against the stone already warmed by the morning sun. One man throws the last few drops of water from his pot against the steps. Another drinks what is left in his pot. None of the water is wasted.

As one who professes himself an atheist it may seem strange that I am giving witness to my being more than a spectator here. This devotion is not only in the hearts and lives of those I am watching this morning. This devotion is in my heart and life. This devotion is mine. I am one of the people I am watching.

Aashish Kumar Chhaturvedi
8 March 2003
Khajuraho

Aashish

Aashish, as you know, I have worked very hard over these last months to effect a regime change in the United States. At this point, only hours before the election, we do not yet have a sense of who will win, though we passionately hope for a Democratic victory as we see the need of a very basic change of direction for the country. This essay, which I sent to many friends and colleagues in the United States and here, some of whom will be angry with my suggestions, will give you a better idea of where I stand these days. You, of course, already know all of this as you and I have talked often in these days. Roger (1 November 2004)

THE STRANGENESS OF AMERICA

> Oh God of earth and alter, bow down and hear our cry.
> Our earthly rulers falter; thy people drift and die.
> The walls of gold entomb us; the swords of scorn divide.
> Take not thy thunder from us, but take away our pride.
>
> **An old Welsh hymn**

My perceptions perhaps heightened by pre-election hysteria in the United States, my other country, I put pen to paper to reflect on the strangeness of that other country which I love and which I know as my other home. Strange, too, that in these twenty-first century days I am using a pen and letter-pad rather than my laptop. Stranger yet that the paper of this letter-pad, purchased in that strange other country, will not take fountain pen ink, so I must use a dot pen (ball point).

Don't get me wrong. I am not inveighing against The United States. I am reflecting from the perspective of one who proudly holds American citizenship and who loves that land, the land of my birth; but who also chooses to live substantial portions of each year in another country, a country which I also love and which has its own strangenesses and challenges. As a global citizen on this quiet Sunday morning I reflect on the overweening, but not unconquerable, challenges that face America now.

In many rational moments I am driven almost to despair by the enormous problems which face my two countries and my world today. The fouled air in which we live, covering the whole of the south Asian continent. Reports that the Iraq war in its first year killed an additional one hundred thousand people, mostly women and children. The horror of genocide in Darfur. The global HIV-Aids crisis, which we here in India are only now just beginning to recognize. I could, of course, go on for pages.

Yet I choose to be an optimist. I choose to move toward a peaceful, happy, prosperous world in which we have dealt with these enormous challenges

Yes, India, too, has its challenges, but none so severe as those facing The United States today. I see three overarching problems which must and which can be solved. I here highlight these by contrasting the American situation with that in India. I list these in order of what I see as their increasing importance, our isolation being the most critical.

First. The problem of Greed. The United States, with about five percent of the world's people, uses twenty-five percent of the world's resources. In India the numbers are just reversed. Twenty-five percent of the world's people use only five percent of the world's resources. We Americans have too much and use too much. Our cars are too big and too many. Most suburban garages are full of the excess stuff which we own. Few Americans use public transportation. Fewer yet walk even enough for their own health. Most Americans are overweight, many obese. We are still super-sizing our meals and drinking massive amounts of cola drinks. Here in India a *chhota* coke – 200 ml – is popular.

Living on a more sustainable, economical, equitable, need I say human, scale, far from being a burden which we must bear, will bring enormous dividends in life satisfaction. We will, all of us and each of us, be the better for it when we find the ways to live within our means on this planet which years ago the space poet Rhysling described, yearning for "the blue-green hills of Earth."

Second. The problem of War. The United States, in its illegal invasion of Iraq, proclaimed a doctrine of pre-emptive strike, maintaining that we have the right to strike first whenever we deem that in our own best interest. We have become the world's biggest and strongest bully. India, on the other hand, though a nuclear nation, has proclaimed a no-first-strike doctrine. We have not and will not strike first. So long as The United States maintains this pre-emptive strike right the rest of the world cringes, like students at recess on the playground, before the enormous military might of Imperial America.

Our world will be a far better place when the nations, led by The United States, turn control of their military arsenals over to The United Nations for use in policing the world. Vast resources will be released for humanitarian development, as only a relatively small police force will be needed.

Last, and most crucial. The problem of Isolation. We Americans live apart from one another. Our families live in small nuclear units, often divided by divorce. We live in massive suburban homes each divided from the next by expanses of lawns, shrubs and trees, or in apartments in which we do not even know the names of the others on the same floor. Here in India most live in extended families and in close daily proximity with their neighbors. There, in America, I've rarely, even in their infancy, held my six grand-children. Here I hold infants nearly every day.

There, in that strange other land which for part of every year I call home, most drivers are alone in their cars every day. I once began counting the cars passing a busy corner at afternoon rush hour. The fifty-seventh car passing that point had three persons in it. The other fifty-six only the driver. Here I rarely see even a scooter or a motor-cycle with less than two or three riders, and most cars and trucks and buses are full.

There are enormous benefits in a life lived together with more people. The ecological benefits, of course, are significant. Five people in one car use far less of the world's petrol than five people each in her/his own car. But the human benefits are much greater. Our lives will be far richer when they are fully integrated with the lives of those around us.

Yes, I find it strange that America, with all her riches, persists in raping the earth. I find it strange that America, with all her goodness, persists in waging war. I find it strange that America, with all her love, persists in living in isolation.

We can and we must and we will move toward a world in which my beloved America leads toward prosperity for all, peace for all, integration for all.

Roger Marley
31 October 2004
Bundelnagar, Kendra Pradesh

Tumhara pyara dost, Roger.

My dear friend Roger Marley shared this essay with me today. He and I are so close in our thinking that I could well have written this myself. I might have been at some pains to be less harsh in my criticism of the

United States as I do not share Roger's situation of being a person with two home countries. India is my home. My essay, had I been the writer, would have focused more on our problems here in *mera pyara bharat*. Though I do believe, as Roger does, that the problems of the United States are much more crucial than those of India.. Aashish (5 November 2004)

----

chhota – small
Tumhara pyara dost – Your dear friend
mera pyara bharat – my beloved India

Mister Chief Minister

How can we be such close friends when everyone in the state and many throughout India know us to be implacable political enemies?

The Chief Minister of Kendra Pradesh, my dear friend and enemy, is one of the most powerful politicians in India. A large, imposing figure who always wears white cotton *khadi,* as I do. His voice, though not strident, is always full and full of conviction. He rarely sits down, preferring to stand, simply as it seems more comfortable to him, not in any way to intimidate others. The strength of his arguments and his smile, do that superbly. He needs no physical props. People listen to him. They pay attention when he speaks.

His face is striking. Not handsome but with chiseled features and piercing eyes. Always clean shaven. Not even a mustache. People who do not know him sometimes surmise that he's a Bollywood hero. He is, in fact, often in front of a camera, though never commercially. Always politically.

He is a bit short of stature, physically. Head and shoulders above the rest, politically. I admire him for that, though I am often at his throat in the heat of political battle.

He has a most engaging smile. One which is not put on or assumed. He genuinely likes people, even those who are implacably set against him, as I so often am. Many a time in what seems absolutely irresolvable controversy he simply smiles at his opponent and wraps up the case.

In short, he's a man to pay attention to.

I always, in public, refer to him as "Mister Chief Minister." He always refers to me either with the honorific Aashish-ji or with my political title when I happen to be in office. I call him "Babloo." – his house-name from childhood -- when sharing a cup of *chai*, or dinner in his home or mine or when enjoying a peg of good Indian whisky. One of the few things on which we agree without any reservation is that Indian whisky is fully as good as Scotch. In private, He calls me by a diminutive of my own name – "Aashi." He picked up this nickname from *Bua,* who in no way approved of our friendship. We would never be so familiar in public. In fact, I think that each of us is a bit proud of the fact that so many people know nothing about this private side of our lives.

How often have we fought, I do not know, in the open, public, political arena. He far to the right and I far to the left. For many years we have engaged in this tug-of-war. Perhaps the very struggle, both in its intensity and in its duration, builds and strengthens the friendship which we have always had for each other, from the moment we first met and realized that, though we were on different sides even in those early political battles, we were drawn to each other in a friendship which has become one of my rich treasures. And yes, one of his also.

I think it is that he and I share a common personal style. Each of us is stubborn -- working toward, dreaming of, and fighting for what we believe in. And each of us is clear about that in which we believe. And. And perhaps this is key. Each of us is willing to pay attention to and listen to the other side or sides in any situation. And there are often many different sides. It is the rare situation which has only two sides. Though I've often suspected, and sometimes accused my friend, "Mister Chief Minister," of recognizing only one side, his own. He laughs and accuses me of similar one-sidedness. Though, of course, each of us recognizes that the one side which we see is not the side at which the other is looking.

In the heat of argument others watching and listening to us often see this one-sidedness and fail to see what he and I never fail to see, that the other's side, or the other sides as is more often the case, has a valid claim to be heard. In the heat of the argument I fight for my side. He staunchly upholds his. And often, though there are many others in the arena, it comes to a stand-off between "Mister Chief Minister" and myself until one or the other steps down off his position and embraces the position of the other – not uncommonly with a physical embrace which surprises those many around us who do not know of our phenomenal personal friendship.

This friendship developed swiftly at a rally in Kanpur years ago in which he was stumping for votes for a local politician. He had risen swiftly in the political sphere and his name easily drew a crowd. I had come to Kanpur because I was strongly against whatever it was he was espousing at that time. I was carrying a placard which identified me as a member of the opposing party and found myself heckling him. He, rather than simply ignoring me or having me thrown out, decided to take me on in the argument. That was so many years ago that I do not remember what it was we argued about. But I remember clearly that I admired his tenacity and his willingness to listen to my heckling. And he has often pointed to that day, and to the shrewdness of my arguments, as the beginning of what has become a lasting and strong friendship.

Though many in our country believe that every politician is a *goonda,* I find that I cannot be that cynical. Surely there are some politicians who rise above the graft and corruption and criminal behavior which sadly is the way of life of most people in politics. My friend, "Mister Chief Minister," again sadly, does nothing to support my belief that not all politicians are *goondas.* He is, as everyone knows, corrupt, involved in graft and crime. In short, my friend is a *goonda,* which, of course, is why *Bua* did not approve of our friendship. I've no fear in labeling him thus. He will not send his goon squads after me. I will not be the victim of a drive-by shooting. Nor will I be pushed in front of a speeding train. On the contrary, his security forces, many of them involved more deeply even than he in criminal behaviour, know me as one of those who, even though deeply opposed to their boss's criminal activity, is on the list of those they protect. Many of them also count me a friend, as I consider them my friends.

Am I at this point simply endorsing criminal behaviour? I think not. It is on many instances of criminal activity where my fights with my friend begin. Often the newspapers, and occasionally the TV news shows us in yet another fight. I am determined to make an honest and law-abiding man of him. He, on his part, is determined to bring me into the mafia system.

In private, over a glass of good Royal Challenge Gold whisky and a plate *of paneer pakoras,* we talk quietly and listen carefully. Rarely does he interrupt me, and rarely do I break into his argument. Only after listening fully to the other do we speak. In public, however, our style is much different. I grew up in the Punjab. I am not a native of Bundelkhand. He has always lived in this notoriously wild and unruly part of Kendra Pradesh. But now and again the newspapers accuse me of having become a *shudh Bundelkhandi* when they find me interrupting, shouting at, gesticulating wildly toward my friend, "Mister Chief Minister," even as he is interrupting me, shouting at me, shaking his fist at me.

Under our bluff and bravado -- perhaps these words are not so well chosen, as our public fights are by no means stage shows, we mean what we say and we are passionate about the positions which we take -- we share a commitment to consensus. Each of us believes that the best way to move ahead is to reach agreement among all those involved in any argument, any situation. We, he and I, are committed to fighting for our personal positions and beliefs until we have either convinced others to come to our position or have listened to and come to theirs. Often, indeed almost always, the final position is neither his initial position nor mine, but some position found by listening not just to each other's but to all other sides. And often we, each of us and those others involved, go away from the arena pleased that we have won. My friend, "Mister Chief Minister," would in no way be pleased to know that we have walked away from the bargaining table with a win on his side and a loss on mine. Nor, and this is key to our strong friendship, nor would I be fully pleased to win at his expense. When, however, he goes away knowing that he has won **and** I have won, then we know that progress has been made. We revel in this reaching of consensus.

In the short run – in the push and shove of every day politics – he and I often go away from the arena or the bargaining table or the conference at odds with the other. Yet each of us lives in the assurance that in the longer run we will reach that consensus, that common agreement, which each of us seeks.

I often laugh when I realize that so few know that "Mister Chief Minister," "Babloo," and I are the best of friends..

Aashish Kumar Chhaturvedi
15 August 2005
Bundelnagar

----

paneer pakoras – a common snack

khadi -- homespun

goonda – criminal, mafia person

shudh Bundelkhandi - a perfect *Bundelkhandi,* a person native to the Bundelkhand region

MY BELOVED COUNTRIES

Such a beautiful country this is,
Such beautiful places –
   Villages and towns and cities.
Such beautiful people –
   Men and women,
   Sons and daughters.
Such a beautiful country this is,
   My country.
   My beloved India.

Such a beautiful country that is,
Such beautiful places –
   Villages and towns and cities.
Such beautiful people –
   Men and women,
   Sons and daughters.
Such a beautiful country that is,
   My other country.
   My beloved America.

Roger Marley
28 September 2005
On a train near Gwalior

Note: I've included this poem because I believe that Father might well have written it had he been a man of two countries as his friend Roger was. Anil

AN INCIDENT ON THE TRAIN

A YOUNG MOTHER, dressed in a simple cotton *sari*, comes and sits on the berth opposite us, her harmonium in her lap. Her little daughter, playing the spoons for rhythm, stands next to her, dressed in a not-overly-dirty frock. The boy, a bit older, carries a drum. The mother sings and plays well. Her children a competent rhythm section.

In the crowded aisle a waiter goes by carrying lunch trays and spills gravy on the girl's frock. She, embarrassed almost to tears, reaches out to her mother who stops playing for a moment to console the girl. Each of them realizing that it might be some days before they are able to wash the dress. I give them three rupees, three times what they usually get.

I sit here in white homespun, Tulsa in a lovely *sari*, clean and comfortable, with many rupees. The mother and her children may collect enough to pay for rice and a few vegetables.

Why do we have so much and they so very little? Surely we are no more deserving than they..

Aashish Kumar Chhaturvedi
15 December 2005
At Shoranur Junction
On The Sabari Express

Purnima at Kanniyakumari

AS *PRITVI* ROLLED slowly toward her, *Chandrama* struggled to rise out of The Bay of Bengal above the sullied haze into the view of the many people waiting for her at this vantage point at the southernmost tip of India where three oceans converge. This haze, most of it a product of humankind's greed and insensitivity, kept the full moon obscured until she was well above the horizon.

We had already seen *Surya* set into the murk to the west above The Arabian Sea.

Today is *Purnima,* and had the air been clear these two would have been very nearly simultaneous events, monthly and marvelous, as they will be again when we humans clean up our planet. We had come to Kanniyakumari especially on this day to see this spectacle.

Now as I write the sky is dark again in the west and *Chandrama* is higher, bright and yellow, in the eastern sky.

Pritvi rolls along; *Chandrama* around her; *Surya* holds both – and all of us – in her pull.

This is *Purnima* at Kanniyakumari in these early days of the twenty-first century, and I am here with my beloved Tulsa..

Aashish Kumar Chhaturvedi
17 December 2005
Kanniyakumari

Purnima - the night of the full moon

Kanniyakumari - literally "virgin goddess";
    an incarnation of Parvati, Lord Shiva's consort;
    and now also the name of the town

Pritvi – Planet Earth

Chandrama – the moon

Surya – the sun

THINK GLOBALLY, ACT GLOBALLY
A manifesto for Rotarians

THE ROTARY CLUB of Kattappana, where I am at the moment (or Addis Ababa, or Emerald City, or any other Rotary club) cares for the world. Our vision, our responsibility, our activity, is for all of humanity, all life, indeed our whole planet. Nothing less will do. We are those who care for the world.

To reject this mandate is to accept the inexorable and inevitable move of the human species into an era of fierce terror – terror not spawned by those we've currently labeled as "terrorists," but terror caused by our own unwillingness to change our ways and to begin to care for every other human being, every other life form – tigers and whales and trees, and each space on the planet -- cities and deserts and the vast oceans, so that we can once again see and revel in "The Blue-Green Hills of Earth."

The seventies and especially the sixties of the previous century were years in which we were urged to "Think Globally, Act Locally." We did indeed act locally as, of course, we must always do. And we told ourselves that we were thinking globally. Far too often, however, we gave only lip service to that part of a very powerful slogan. In fact, we cared only for our own area, our own Rotary district, our own country, people of our own color or class or religion. We failed, in most instances, to pick up the responsibility which is our natural heritage, our responsibility for all the world in all its myriad manifestations.

It is not simply a poetic nicety to affirm that the hunger of a child in Darfur is my hunger. In fact, if a child anywhere is starving, I am starving.

I must, of course, feed myself and my family. But a larger, stronger, more basic mandate is my responsibility to feed the world. Indeed, the people of the world are my family.

I sit at this moment on a ridge of The Western Ghats, the range separating the state of Kerala from the state of Tamil Nadu, in southern India. On a lovely spring day. We look down into the Cumbum valley and, because of the pall of smog which for several years now has covered the Indian subcontinent, we cannot see across the valley. Yet we refuse to see the filthy air in which we live simply because here in the high ranges it is somewhat cleaner.

We live in a world in which fully one quarter of our family members lack pure drinking water.

As those who care for the whole world and for all of humankind we must deal with these and a host of other problems from a global perspective, and our activity must be global. We must THINK GLOBALLY AND ACT GLOBALLY.

To accept this mandate is not complex. Indeed it is amazingly simple. Calculate the amount of Earth's resources available to each human being and organization and require each to live within that limit or to pay a reasonable tax allowing him or her to use more. – that tax to be used to provide an extra measure of sustainable resources (perhaps in hectares reforested).

To accept this mandate will not be difficult for those here and around the world who are already living a simple, sustainable life style.

To accept this mandate will, however, be enormously difficult for those of us, that small minority of the world's people, who are living a profligate life style far beyond the means of the planet. We will have to scale back drastically, using only a small portion of the global resources we now consume. This will be a colossal challenge.

To accept this mandate, though, will in the end provide a better, happier, more fulfilling life for all. For those who are now wealthy and privileged as surely as for those who are now destitute.

It may well prove too difficult for the Rotarians of this generation -- people of wealth and privilege and responsibility – to accept this mandate. Surely, however, it is not too much to hope that these five boys who have come up here with us today – boys of wealth and privilege and responsibility – will pick up the challenge.

That one day all people on this "blue-green" planet will live free and secure. That one day the vast resources of Planet Earth will sustain the people of Planet Earth. That one day "tigers [will again] roam the forests and great whales roam the seas.."

Aashish Kumar Chhaturvedi
11 February 2011
Kattappana, Kerala

WE WON

from Anil's Journal
10 Sept 2016

Yes! At last we did it! No, I don't mean Yes! India won. We often do that, and we are of course celebrating that. We'd expected that victory. What I mean is

Yes! At last we've succeeded in getting Father out of India. We won.

Nobody who knew him ever questioned his loyalty to India. He, from the time of his election to the Nagar Panchayat of Bundelnagar, that grubby refugee camp where I was born, right through to today, his ninetieth birthday, has been respected and recognized as one of India's leading citizens. Sought after by more than one president and several prime ministers, and often a staunch advisor to Kendra Pradesh's chief minister (when Congress was in power there). He had no aspirations to political offices higher than the local level – not even on the state level. But his voice was heard and listened to by many, even by his political rivals.

Whenever we suggested a trip abroad – perhaps just a vacation trip to Europe or a shopping trip to Dubai – he would laugh and say, "Why should I go abroad? Everything I want and need is right here in India." So we've been scheming and cajoling for years trying to find a chink in his patriotic armor. And finally we found that chink – cricket.

It's a moot point whether Father's love for cricket is stronger than his love for India or whether Father's love for India is stronger than his love for cricket. In any event, he knows all the players, knows the scores of many of the matches over the years, knows how many centuries each of our batsmen has scored. One of the finest weekends of his life was the weekend some years back when Sachin Tendulkar had been a guest in our home. Father had of course met and talked with him often and Sachin took the opportunity of their friendship to come to Bundelnagar and to our home for a few days resting up after a strenuous series of test matches in which he had scored three centuries.

We're here in Colombo now celebrating – as we expected to – India's victory over Pakistan in a 20/20 match. Father, of course, grumbled a bit about this new cricket format which has been so popular for the past decade or so. Though he liked the one day format of fifty overs per innings, he thought this a much too truncated form of the game. He would have been pleased to have come here for a test match and would have been in the stands for the whole three or four days.

This outing – can one call an overseas trip, a trip out of the country, a trip to "foreign", indeed the only trip abroad that Ashish Kumar Chhaturvedi has ever taken, an "outing?" Let's rather call it an "Event." This "Event" was a gift from Father's best friend (and political rival) "Mr. Chief Minister" (Yes, the BJP is back in power in Kendra Pradesh and Prem Agarwal is again our chief minister). "Aashi, " he had said, using the diminutive with which he addressed Father in private, "let's go to Colombo for the 20/20 match next month. With our presence -- yours and mine – India surely will beat those Pakistanis. It will be your ninetieth birthday. What say, shall we go?" To my surprise – we'd been making such requests and suggestions so often over the years to no avail – Father said, "Oh, all right, Babloo," using the house-name with which he addressed the Chief Minister in private, "I guess it is time I got out of the country for awhile."

I always called father "Father." Even when he was reprimanding me and talking sternly with me, addressing me as "Anil Chhaturvedi" rather than simply as "Anil" or "Son." He, for his part, unfailingly addressed his father, my grandfather, *mera dada,* as *"Pita-ji",* the Hindi word for "father" with the honorific *"-ji"* added.

Jet Airways had put on a special flight direct nonstop from Khajuraho to Colombo for this cricket match, so the party started there in the Khajuraho airport even before the flight. Arriving in the Colombo airport Father headed for the duty-free shop. "What, Aashi, are you going to buy some Johnnie Walker Black Label for our celebration?" the Chief Minister asked.

"No," Father replied, "Of course not. Would I drink Scotch whisky? I'll pick up a couple of bottles of

ROYAL CHALLENGE *GOLD* A BLEND OF RARE SCOTCH AND MATURED INDIAN MALT WHISKIES."

"It's bad enough that they even mention "rare Scotch" on the label, but," he sighed, "we still have not gotten enough gumption to assert that our Indian whisky is every bit as good as Scotch."

Everyone knows, of course, that the amount of Scotch whisky is miniscule – we've still not adopted any regulations concerning the minimum amount permissible. The only reason that there is any Scotch whisky in these bottles at all – if there is any at all – is so that people will think they are drinking good whisky. I agree with Father and with "Mr. Chief Minister" that it is time we stood up for our Indian products. "*Swadeshi* whisky," I cry. "No more IMFL (Indian Made Foreign Liquor). lets have IMIL (Indian Made Indian Liquor)."

We won the match. Not easily. It was well played by both teams. Ganguly was bowled out in the second over and Sachin was caught out early in our innings. We ended the innings with a score of 98 for 4, a tough target for the Pakistani team, but not an unreachable one. Some brilliant batting by the Pakistanis and a couple of missed balls by our fielders, brought us to the last ball of the match with a score of 98 for India, 92 for Pakistan. A *chauka* (four runs) would have tied the match. A *chukka* (six runs) would have given them the victory.

Their batsman muffed that last chance and we won.

We went to the locker room, of course, after the match, and congratulated our team. Sachin was surprised to see Father there. He had known of Father's reluctance – indeed, refusal – to leave India.

Then back to our hotel for our own private celebration. As it turned out one of Minister Agarwal's Sri Lankan friends had met us at the airport and presented him with a welcoming bottle of Sri Lankan Mahua, so we drank the best local *toddy* instead of Indian whisky.

Now Father is asleep, as I will be myself soon. How good it is to travel with this man who is my beloved father. How proud I am to be by his side when others greet us. And how much fun it is to have finally won our long fought battle with him and brought him – though only just barely out of India – to "foreign."

WORLD PEACE AND UNDERSTANDING

KEYNOTE ADDRESS TO THE SECOND WORLD'S PARLIAMENT OF RELIGIONS, KHAJURAHO, INDIA, 14 FEBRUARY 2018

MERE PYARE BHAIYO aur benino, my dear brothers and sisters, I am here this morning to celebrate with you a stupendous turning point in world history. This conference stands at a point at which the peoples of the world are turning from decades, centuries, millennia of wars and suspicion to a remarkable level of tranquility and harmony.

As many of you know, I have been a Rotarian most of my adult life, and as many of you also know I believe Rotary International has been for the past more than a century the strongest **secular** force for world peace and understanding. So I take these words from Rotary – World Peace and Understanding – as my topic this morning.

There is, though, another, and perhaps even stronger, force bringing us to this point. Bringing us into a future alive with the possibilities of a world which lives in peace and understanding.

Mere pyare bhaiyo aur benino, I refer, of course, to you. The strongest force is, I believe, the **religious** force, that force which is the deepest personal motivation of every human life, that force which you represent here today.

Some of you are, I know, wondering how it is that a professed atheist, myself, has been chosen as the keynoter of a conference on religion. Surely this fellow is in the wrong conference, many are saying. Indeed, many are not in attendance at all, feeling that this conference is too ecumenical in affirming all world religions, in fact going further than that as my presence apparently attests. I refer sadly to many of our fundamentalist brothers and sisters, mostly conservative Christians and Muslims, and also sadly to those in this country who are in the fundamentalist wings of Hinduism.

There are also, though, several delegates to this conference who are not in this hall. Some of them simply stayed away. Some are right outside the hall actively protesting my presence here. I spoke with several of those people this morning, many of them my friends.

Why, then, am I here? I was, frankly, a bit surprised at the invitation. Though I believe that I am the right person to address you here this morning. As I talk with you briefly about consensus and about reaching into The Collective Consciousness I hope you will agree.

In any event, it is with deep personal pleasure that I address you this morning, and I ask you to hear me now with the same respect in which I hold each of you, my dear brothers and sisters.

It so often seems, as it seemed to most at the turn of this century, that any kind of positive, progressive future for the planet or for the individual is not possible without something from outside ourselves.

The events of these past eighteen years show that this pessimism is simply misplaced. Human beings have within themselves, individually and especially collectively, all that they need. No outside help – and here I know many of you will challenge me, and perhaps I am wrong. No outside help has been needed to bring us to this glorious period in the life of Planet Earth. We are coming into a time in human history in which we reach into The Collective Consciousness of Earth's people, the aggregate of all human consciousness, to find consensus on a global scale and a consensus which is being reached in innumerable smaller instances.

What is it that has made this global and local consensus possible? What has turned human society on this planet so radically around? How is it that we no longer treat one another as enemies and competitors but as fellow citizens on Planet Earth? I see four factors, four reasons, four dynamics. And perhaps a fifth.

The "unthinkable" was becoming possible, indeed seemingly inevitable. At the turn of the century more countries were building or planning or hoping for nuclear arsenals. It seemed to many only a matter of time before a nuclear holocaust would occur on Planet Earth. World leaders and the population at large found this simply untenable. We decided, collectively and in many individual instances of consensus, to gain control of this monster so that we no longer needed to fear a nuclear conflagration which might have wiped out all life on the planet. This began with the work of General Amir of Pakistan and his counterpart here in India. When these two military leaders reached consensus and then when they included their nation's leaders in that consensus it was found possible to turn their not inconsiderable nuclear arsenals over to complete United Nations control. This conference is now being held in a nuclear-free zone – the south Asian continent.

Other nations seeing this momentous breakthrough in Pakistan/India relations are now beginning to move together, reaching agreements on issues between countries, issues which had seemed intractable. Palestine and Israel quickly followed Pakistan and India. One by one other nations are turning their nuclear armaments over to United Nations control. The United States, whom many feared would never relinquish these enormous weapons, is now very close to doing just that. These steps are leading to the bringing down of the military establishments in every country as each country realizes that they need only a small police force. The security of the people of the world will no longer be guaranteed by national force, but will be in the hands of The United Nations Police.

We have taken enormous steps. We now find ourselves taking many smaller ones as well. The freeing up of financial resources no longer needed to maintain individual national armed forces enables us to tackle other problems which had seemed unsolvable. This is leading to a world of abundance in which we are finally finding a more equitable distribution of the world's resources and the elimination of severe poverty.

A third major factor in bringing to fruition the vision of Collective Consciousness has been the growth of the information society in which we live. This began with the development of the internet and the ease of communication around the world. As people learned more about other people in the world we began to listen to one another and to honor one another. We realized, in other words, that consensus serves us better than confrontation. And since we no longer had vast military means of confrontation we turned to consensus in our dealings with one another.

The fourth major factor is a milestone which we expect to reach in just three more years, with the leveling of Earth's population at around eight billion people.

And there may be one more factor. Perhaps we were simply tired. Tired of fighting one another. And we decided, collectively, in the words of the old spiritual, "[We] ain't gonna study war no more. [We] ain't gonna study war no more." We live now in peace and understanding and prosperity on Planet Earth.

Let me now, *mere pyare bhaiyo aur benino,* take this opportunity to announce publicly and for the first time the momentous plans which are afoot right here and which in about fifteen years time will come to fruition very close to this spot.

Just across the Rajnagar Road from this conference centre, next to the Chitragupta Temple, a new temple is to be constructed. This will be very similar in construction to the Chitragupta Temple, utilizing the same building techniques and being built also of Panna sandstone. This temple will honor all peoples and especially their religious strivings. It is to be dedicated to Lord Shiva as is its counterpart, the Matangeshwar Temple just across the temple compound. It is our hope that people will worship here every day for the next thousand years as they have every day for the past thousand years at the Matangeshwar Temple. Both temples will be open at all times. The new temple will be known as *Janata Mandir,* the Temple of the Peoples.

It is with deep respect and love now that I welcome all, *mere pyare bhaiyo aur benino,* my dear brother's and sisters, to this Second World's Parliament of Religions.

I close now with words with which our Muslim brothers and sisters often bless each other in parting: *khuda hafiz..*

Aashish Kumar Chhaturvedi
14 February 2018
Khajuraho Conference Centre

Aashish

from Anil's Journal
21 February 2018

The Second World's Parliament of Religions has come to a celebrative close, ending a week of sharing such as the world has never known. This sort of religious amity would simply not have been possible even ten years ago. Much has happened in these past ten years as the world's people have moved by leaps and bounds toward a new era of peace and understanding.

Father had not been the organizer of this conference. He and his dear friend Kiran Verma, poet laureate of Khajuraho, had suggested the conference to the leadership of the Vivekananda Kendra in Kanniyakumari after Father and *Mata-ji* had visited Kanniyakumari in 2005. They had been so struck then with the message and witness of Vivekananda that they joined the Vivekananda Kendra and with Kiran Verma began working toward a Second World's Parliament of Religions. The conference was then organized as a follow-up, 125 years after the 1893 conference in Chicago at which Swami Vivekananda had delivered that stupendous address. India was chosen as the host country as India was swiftly coming into the ranks of developing nations, India has an ancient tradition of religious ecumenism, and India is the home of Swami Vivekananda. And Khajuraho was chosen as the site of the conference.

The week-long conference was hugely successful, drawing delegates from most of the world's religious traditions. There were, of course, elements (mostly fundamentalist) in Christianity and Islam who stayed away, still insisting that their way was the only true way. The Shiv Sena also loudly denounced the conference. Nevertheless, even these were represented by senior (though without official credentials) members who came mostly because of Father's invitation. They knew him and respected him, though they were far from agreement with him.

Ten years ago the much vaunted War on Terror, led by the bullying forces of the United States, had come to a resounding close with the nations realizing that this negative approach would never bring world peace. This country and our close friend and ally, Pakistan, have now taken the momentous step of turning control of our nuclear arsenals over to the United Nations and steps are being taken toward UN control of nuclear weapons of all the world's nations. This has been one of Father's fondest dreams. And yesterday, at the conclusion of the conference, the chairman spoke of this possibility and hope.

It is Father's dream, and the substance of much of his work over the last quarter of a century, that national armies will be disbanded, that major armed force in this world will be in the hands of the United Nations.

Father had been asked to deliver the keynote address, and this almost demands a bit of commentary, as Father was an atheist. Father never was a religious man, though he would have called himself a Hindu in his earlier years. The horror of the events of Partition, his mother's and his sister's deaths then, and the larger carnage of those days, much of it spawned by communal tension between Hindus and Muslims, was perhaps the strongest trigger toward his rejection of organized religion. His study over the years led to his personal stance. He himself often said, often in these very words, "I believe that there is no supreme being to whom we owe some sort of allegiance." Clearly more than the statement of one who himself does not believe in God. Rather the statement of one who believes that there is no God. A thoroughgoing, unequivocal atheist.

He was widely recognized as a secular humanist. And people knew that he not only advocated decision making by consensus, but actively pursued this method of human interaction. And, as he said so clearly in his keynote address, he believed that consensus was seeking the understanding of Collective Consciousness, the aggregate wisdom of the group making the decision and ultimately the collected wisdom of all sentient beings. Many of his friends asserted that this was just his way of defining his own belief in God. Father simply laughed with them and said, "No, I am an atheist. I believe that there is no God."

It was at the World's Parliament, in his address, that he officially presented the plan for the new temple in Khajuraho. He and Kiran Verma had already done a great deal of planning and had conferred with government and other people in Khajuraho and in the central government, and especially with officials of the Archeological Survey of India here in Khajuraho.

The plan is to build a new temple next to the Chitragupta Temple on the site of the stage of the Khajuraho Festival of Dances. The new temple is to be the same height and with the same basic dimensions as the Chitragupta Temple, but is to be of modern design. It will be built with the same stone and the same building techniques as the other temples. To be named *janata mandir,* the Temple of the Peoples. It will be a temple dedicated to Lord Shiva, in keeping with most of the other temples here, but with prominent representations of the other major world religions in the architecture. It is to be open to everyone always. It is to be hoped that this temple, on the north side of the Western Group, will be consecrated for the next thousand years, as the Matangeshwar Temple, on the south side, has been consecrated for the past thousand; that people will worship at these two temples for another millennium.

Aashish

THE LIGHT HAS gone out of my life. Tulsa is dead.

Meri priyatum bibi, how will I go on without you? To say nothing about joy and fun and love and zest for life, how will I even take one more breath?

You have been with me and by my side for so very long now. We have known each other now nearly one hundred years. Since *Bua* took me, a boy of only four, to your home on the very day of your birth. She knew that she had planned our marriage and I suppose that she talked on and on to me then about it, though I remember nothing of that day itself. My earliest memories, though, are of playing together when we were children. *Bua* made it abundantly clear very early that we were made for each other and that our marriage had all but been arranged since even before your birth.

Now you are gone. And my life is dark.

Many there are who see me as a strong individual. Few, though, know that you are so often the source of my strength.

Your strength flowed to me so fully in the time of our flight from Alimabad. We were newlyweds then and Mother's death had thrown the mantle of family leadership onto my shoulders. You held me in the shuddering agony of those days.

In later years, when in the heat of political controversy, especially with my dear friend Babloo, I have come home exhausted and wondering how I was to carry on, you have come to me with a glass of *chai* and assurance of your love and support. Even on those times when you were siding with Babloo.

Yes, Tulsa, *meri priyatum bibi,* I can prepare my own *chai..*

Aashish Kumar Chhaturvedi
16 May 2024
Bundelnagar

Mata-ji died swiftly of a massive stroke. She had gone into the kitchen after lunch. Father heard a crash and ran to see what had happened. She was lying on the floor. She spoke briefly then lapsed into unconsciousness and died even before medical help could come. Her body was cremated that evening and father wrote his last journal entry.

With this brief entry with its silly comment about *chai* Father ended the journal he had begun on their wedding night. Perhaps it is appropriate that he wrote nothing more in his personal journal after *Mata-ji's* death.

The *chai* comment, though, reveals clearly that Father intended to go on with his life. He lived a bit more than ten years longer and in that time witnessed – indeed, was a significant force in bringing about -- two historic events:

>--the declaration of Planet Earth as a nuclear free zone in 2028, and
>--the dedication of the Janata Mandir in Khajuraho in 2033.

He moved to Khajuraho shortly after *Mata-ji's* death, where he lived with Kiran Verma's family. Anil

A NUCLEAR FREE EARTH

From Anil's Journal
6 August 2030

Father would surely have commented on the events of this day – momentous events in the history of the world and events in whose coming about he surely played a role, for he was a man of peace, a peacemaker – but he had made a clear decision to end writing after Mata-ji's death. I urged him to break his silence this time. He steadfastly refused. He was a stubborn man. So, here are my poor comments on this great day:

Earlier today in a simple ceremony at United Nations headquarters the President of the United States handed a key to the Prime Minister of Japan who then gave it to the President of the United Nations who then declared:

Planet Earth, now and from this day forward, is a nuclear free zone. Control of all Earth's nuclear armaments is now in the hands of the United Nations. Never again will these awesome weapons be used.

Today marks the eighty-fifth anniversary of the first use of nuclear weapons in warfare. This is the anniversary of the dropping of an atomic bomb on the city of Hiroshima by a plane of the Army Air Corps of the United States of America. That bombing and the dropping of another atomic bomb on a different Japanese city a few days later mark the only time that nuclear weapons have been used in warfare. In handing that symbolic key to the Prime Minister of Japan the President of the United States formally ended a blot on the relationship between those two great nations.

Intense diplomacy and negotiations had been required to bring us to the point of living in a nuclear free zone. Beginning with the relinquishing of control of their nuclear arsenals by India and Pakistan, nation after nation gave these awesome weapons to the United Nations. The United States, the world's first, today became its last nuclear power.

Father had been increasingly called upon for his counsel, particularly after the delivery and publication of the Keynote address at the Second World Parliament of Religions. More and more leaders recognized the power of consensus, which he had so compellingly spelled out in that address, and it was only through consensus that this day finally was possible.

My father, Aashish Kumar Chhaturvedi, was a driving force toward this momentous shift in the way in which Earth's people live together.

From Anil's Journal
21 March 2033

Father walked slowly to the podium and delivered these remarks in a voice shaking sometimes with emotion, sometimes with age. He is one-hundred-six years old. Still vigorous and active. This was the last time he spoke in public, and the last written words which I have found in his papers. Anil.

DEDICATION OF THE *JANATA MANDIR*, KHAJURAHO

Remarks of Aashish Kumar Chhaturvedi, Chief Guest

With deep respect and love I greet you all, *mere pyare bhaiyo aur behino,* my beloved brothers and sisters. We are here this evening to dedicate this magnificent temple honouring people of faith from the many different traditions. Kiran Verma's poem, which you heard earlier, affirms this world as a world in which "all people know you as the one God though we still worship you in richly diverse forms." And as I look out over this great crowd tonight I revel in our richly divergent faiths.

I had the privilege of reading Kiran's poem several days ago. I live, after all, in his home. And I've been troubled by that assertion. It is patently not true. There are those who would not subscribe to it, believing that their own limited understanding is somehow the final truth. There are those in this world who hold tenaciously to their own fundamentalist beliefs and who will not rejoice with us here in the Temple of the Peoples.

How, then, does Kiran make this ringing affirmation? This statement of a deeper truth? I've been brought to understanding through the prescient theology of the Apostle Paul in the Christian scriptures. Paul affirms two great theological verities – salvation and reconciliation. Salvation, God's great work, is achieved, finished, complete. Reconciliation, our work, is far from complete. We have a great deal still to do.

Much of my life has been devoted to the work of reconciliation, and we in this world have reached some phenomenal milestones in this global work. I briefly mention only three, and there are many many more.

- Fifteen years ago, right here in Khajuraho, we held the Second World's Parliament of Religions.

- Eight years ago the South Asian Economic Union was chartered.
- Three years ago, with the control of United States atomic weapons turned over to the United Nations we have declared this world a Nuclear Free Zone.

Now in the dedication of The *Janata Mandir* we accept the continuing work of reconciliation in large arenas and small. Most importantly we carry forward this work as we reach out to individuals and groups who are not represented here tonight. May the witness of this temple be that God is one, though we know Him by many names. To quote Gandhi-ji's favorite *bhajan:* "*Ishwar, Allah, tera nam.*" *Khuda Hafiz..*

Janata Mandir – the Temple of the Peoples
bhajan – a devotional song
Ishwar, Allah, tera nam –
    Ishwar (Hindu name for God),
    Allah (Muslim name for God),
    tera nam – your name
Khuda Hafiz – a common Muslim parting salutation meaning, May Allah protect you.

Aashish

ALWAYS

THE RAIN FALLS gently again tonight
And there is no wind.
But in the skies above Khajuraho
Great sheets of lightning and jagged forks
Announce the beauty of your dance,
Lord Shiva.

SURELY YOU ARE pleased with your people.
Yet again You are dancing in the night sky.
Tonight You revel with us in this,
Your temple, honouring the people of the whole earth.

REJOICING IN A world in which
Abundant food, clean air, safe drinking water
Are being made available to all.
Where lakes and streams and rivers
Are being cleaned up;
Where tigers soon will roam the forests,
And great whales again will roam the seas;
A world in which health care is freely available to all;
Where everyone has a safe and secure home in which to live;
A world in which music and dance and the arts are flourishing;
And every person has access to superb education;
Where all people know You as the One God,
Though we still worship You in richly diverse forms.

OFTEN YOU HAVE come to us, in outward show,
Lord Shiva,
In the clash and furor of the storm,
Phir bhi hamesha hamare dil main tu nachta hai.
Yet always in our hearts You dance..

Kiran Verma
21 March 2033 CE
at the dedication of
The Temple of The Peoples
Annual Dance Festival
Khajuraho, India

from Anil's Journal
10 September 2034

Father died today. A most auspicious day. His 108th birthday.

We've known for some months that he was failing. Every evening of his life he has gone to the temple for *darshan,* climbing slowly up the twenty-seven steps, pausing briefly to touch Ganesha's feet, going on up to ring the great bell, going round the side and up the inside back steps to the platform, coming round to kneel before the great stone *lingam,* touching his forehead to the stone pavement in reverence, receiving three spoonfuls of *gangajal* from the *pujari,* and a red *tilak* of blessing, standing with palms joined in *namaste* through the brief and glorious *arati* – the clanging of gongs, the waving of a lamp, the blowing of trumpet and conch.

It was at the beginning of this year's monsoon that we began carrying Father up to the temple each evening. Still he always looked for his friends the flower-girls and bought a *mala* for blessing, giving a ten rupee coin in exchange for the same sort of garland which he used to buy from their grandmother, Salu, for one rupee, and from her mother before that and even earlier from Salu's grandmother when I was only an infant when we first came to Bundelnagar. I suppose that in those days he paid only an anna or two. They were still on the old system of coinage then. How many garlands did Father buy from this family?

For how many annas? How many paise? From five generations of flower-girls over almost ninety years.

Yesterday Father did not go for *darshan*. He was too weak even to be carried. And today the flower-girls sold nothing to the tourists. All their flowers, basketsful of them, bedecked Father's corpse in their own tribute to his love and friendship.

We carried his body wrapped in white cotton *khadi* to the old burning *ghat* at the riverside. Only for the most important people do we go back to the old ways of a sandalwood pyre on the riverbank. For Father this was appropriate. For many years he has been acknowledged as Bundelnagar's and then as Khajuraho's leading citizen.

Father never gained high political office because he refused to be involved in the corruption, the deceit, the deception which too often accompany political progress; and because his concern and his work always was for the common people, people of the villages, and for his students and family.

It is a hot September evening. I have fulfilled all my ritual functions as the eldest, indeed the only, son. Father's life has been lived. And lived very well. Now it is done.

Many were here for the final rituals. Now all have gone. I am alone. Alone simply with the burning embers and the ashes and my own thoughts of my beloved Father. Though he never rose politically higher than local government, yet he was widely known, even internationally, as a man of peace and wisdom. He was admired by all who knew him and loved by those who knew him best. Most of all he was loved by Tulsa, his wife of nearly eighty years, and by his children and grandchildren.

Many of his acquaintances thought him a *jivanmukta,* one who has achieved liberation while still in this life. His closest friends and family knew better. As the old saying goes, *"insan hi to he,"* "he is only a man." Aashish Kumar Chhaturvedi was an ordinary man, though one deeply loved.

Anil Chhaturvedi
10 September 2034
Khajuraho

----

darshan – being in the presence of holiness

lingam – representation of Lord Shiva

gangajal – holy water from River Ganga

pujari – worship leader

tilak – mark of blessing on forehead

namaste -- greeting

arati – celebrative worship

mala – garland

khadi – homespun

burning *ghat* – place of cremation

ISBN 141209982-X